Nicholas House is a British born wri
South of England. He took up writir
by the stories of Jules Verne and H.C

Fascinated by the natural world he v
university. This afforded him the chance to travel and fuel his over
active imagination, allowing him to take inspiration from a vast
array of varied sources.

He went on to merge his passion for writing and love for video
production by creating scripted videos on YouTube which continues
to let him experiment with a variety of writing styles.

Primarily writing Supernatural Fantasy and Science Fiction,
Nicholas has also written numerous pieces of published poetry
alongside short stories, e-books and scientific articles. With a mind
so full of ideas and an ongoing literary passion he plans to continue
writing about whatever inspires him long into the future.

Also by Nicholas House

Novels
Chronicles of the Median

Novellas
The Dark
Illumination

Collections
Abridged: A Short Collection of Short Stories

The Median

Nicholas House

The Median
Copyright© 2011, 2022 Nicholas House

<u>Contents</u>

Prologue - The City of Light

Then I saw a great white throne and him who was seated on it. Earth and sky fled from his presence and there was no place for them

-Revelations 21:11

Mankind's affliction with the physical and the spiritual has surpassed what anyone could have expected. Nations wage wars for the supposed 'Glory of God' in vein attempts to obtain their deity's grace. No-one ever supposes that they are fighting for the wrong side, plunging themselves ever deeper into the satanic flames.

Evil has always existed, not in the form of a devil or land of flaming brimstone but in people. People's greed and lust for power fuels deeds that shouldn't even be conceived of let alone carried out. An evil such as this can spread beyond life and if the will is strong enough, grow beyond control. Accepted should be the fact that it is futile to speculate about the next world. Is there an afterlife? Heaven? Hell? The true question is 'What lies between?' A ghost world? Some kind of nether plane, where the restless dead await their passage to the gleaming city of light, or await their trial and judgement. None the less, no matter where, the evil of man will rule out and tyranny of the worlds hate will consume.

There are those who know things. Things about the Earth and beyond that should never be known. Most of these few people refuse to believe it all to be real and the even fewer who do don't care to acknowledge it at all. Those few who do the truths are oppressed and dismissed by the masses and their 'righteous' religions as kooks and members of the occult. These people, though, are strong. Their abilities can place them in situations where reality can seem like a dream and dreams like nightmares. Still, the naive are at risk, the weak and the inexperienced. They can be seen as portals, unguarded gates by those longing to return from the Other Side, and are readily open to possession by powerful spirits with a long history in the Median world. However, instances of possession are rare and are dealt with as much due care as they deserve, sometimes hidden as extreme cases of Dissociative Personality Disorder.

Like they can travel to our world, we too are able to cross the silent borders that divide our planes. But only the most skilled of Medians may do this at will without fear of the shadows which stalk them. These instances, though, are even rarer than possessions and are not only looked upon by most with speculation but a great air of impossibility. It is unlikely that Medians can physically control the dearly departed; to do this would require a power far greater than anyone has ever possessed, rather they merely commune with them, ease their concerns about what comes next. Medians exist solely to guide the lonely dead to their spiritual destiny with as little disturbance to the world at large as possible. Maintaining the illusion that the unknown beyond remains exactly that. But on occasions restless souls will make themselves known and the Medians purpose is called upon for much more than its original intentions.

I - A Long Night

Absent in body, but present in spirit

-Corinthians 5:3

As a child I was never a large believer in anything other than what I knew to be true. As far as I was concerned, that was simply the world around me. There were dreams, though. Every child has nightmares but these were different; terrible visions of what I was sure couldn't be real. My parents always told me that I had an overactive imagination. How could they understand when they never even wanted to try? What's worse is that I believed them. At least up until that night.

I was only twelve. I had always been scared of driving in the rain. The noise. Not being able to see what was out there. But then our car was run off the road by a jack-knifing lorry and...No one should have to see that sort of thing, let alone a child when his parents are involved. There was only one thing that could have been worse and that was to live though it twice. In my dreams I had already seen it, every harrowing detail yet the very essence of what I had been taught told me not to accept it. For the next few months I lived with my aunt and every day wrestled to come to terms with everything that I had lived though, all the time experiencing more and more vivid visions. Amazing places constructed of what was almost pure light, shadowy figures and an ever present feeling that I was not like the others. Eventually I accepted that I could no longer go on *denying that which was so obvious. I had something, a gift, and to deny it would bring something that wasn't even worth thinking about.*

Sure, I'd been christened...Haven't we all? But it's not as though I liked the religion, bunch of hypocrites if you ask me. It's safe to say that I try to keep as far away from any sort of church as I can. It must be some sort of cruel irony of fate, then, that those happen to be the first place they always think of heading.

The dull, sodium yellow of a flickering streetlamp fell upon the single car parked beneath, it's light doing nothing to warm the cold, wet street. Sat within, motionless, a dark figure watched shimmering silhouettes against the strained glass of the old stone chapel adjacent.

After a minute or two he abruptly opened the car door and swung a leg out into the drizzling rain. He paused and looked to the gloomy October sky, then back down and shook his head. He continued to exit the car and slammed the door, causing a torrent of water beads to run forward from the sunroof onto the windscreen. Pulling forward his leather jacket and adjusting the collar in a vain attempt to protect from the rain, he began to stride towards the chapels large door.

He grabbed the iron handle and listened though the wood to what sounded like a scuffle, or at least a one sided struggle. Eventually the doors were pushed open and he entered briskly, leaving a drizzly mist in his wake.

Inside, two youths were attempting to pull a poor box from the clenched arms of a clergyman.

"Hey!"

The youths quickly turned around and gritted their teeth, with one stepping forward and flicking his own collar up aggressively.

"Wha' du ya want!?" this was barked as though it were a command, despite there being no authority to command with.

"I would like you to leave..." the man looked them both up and down in turn, "right now," he began to walk forward, slowly sliding his hand inside his jacket.

"And 'ow ya gunna make us!?" the second youth snapped, squeezing the tip of his cap together and spitting on the ground.

"I said now." He smoothly drew a long barrelled six round revolver from a holster concealed under his glistening wet leather jacket and pointed it casually at the nearest youth. "I suggest you comply," he finished after a few seconds.

The youths shuffled uneasily and then started towards the door. The barrel of the gun tracked them out of the chapel and then began to fall as the door creaked to a close.

The priest stood, unsure whether to be pleased by the actions of this mysterious individual or appalled. Before he had a chance to speak the chamber of the gun was quickly flicked open. Its sharp click made the cleric jump and a voice came from behind the still dripping leather as the revolver was brought into open view.

"Don't worry…It's not loaded," the chamber was flicked back into place and the weapon was replaced into its holster.

"Thank you, my child," the priest spoke at last and loosened his grip on the poor box as the stranger slowly turned around. "What is your name?"

"As if it matters…" he once again straightened his jacket and then looked directly at the priest "Weignright…My name is Richard Weignright," his voice discerned itself as soft yet with an oddly distant texture followed by a quality described only by that of an echo. His general appearance seemed to perfectly match his voice. He was clean shaven and his thick black hair fell loosely into whatever style it appeared to see fit with flecks of his fringe tumbling about his brow.

"Thank you, Richard," the priest reached a free hand forward in order to distribute a blessing but it was quickly pushed away.

"Don't think you can thank me yet," he looked around the chapel altar carefully. Two large candles burnt steadily, their light partially reflected by the polished brass cross at the centre of the arrangement. Suddenly the candles flicked violently in quick succession, right to left. Richard looked back to the clergyman. "You'd better leave me to it. It may get…" he sought for the correct word and eventually settled on something that was reasonably acceptable, "interesting."

He seemed largely taken aback by the proposal. "Leave you to what?" he didn't expect an answer but briefly waited for one none the less. "This is my chapel and if I didn't have those youngsters telling me what to do, I certainly will not have you doing so!" he breathed and seemed pleased with his sermon.

Richard quickly glanced to the heavens. "Fine. Suit yourself," he began to slowly walk towards the alter, the candles continuing to flick back and forth as he stepped up. The flickering abruptly ceased and became isolated to the left candle. He leant towards the flame, the flickering growing more aggressive as he did so, and felt an odd chill surround him. It took it upon itself to ignore any concept of flesh and bite directly at Richards bone.

The priest craned his neck in an attempt to gain a concept of what kind of ritual was taking place. "What are you doing?" he finally inquired cautiously but was completely ignored.

Richard looked deeper into the fire, then abruptly closed his eyes. He whispered some inaudible verse before sharply blowing at the candle, extinguishing the dancing flame. He opened his eyes again and slowly swivelled them around. Gradually a breeze began to pick up and he nodded to himself, acknowledging the fact as though it had been spoken. The breeze only grew as he stepped down from the altar and took up a position in front of it.

The clergyman began to panic as a gust of wind swept in and extinguished the candles dotted around the building. The only light that was left was that of the misty moon and street lights outside. It filtered in streaks through the stained glass, tainting the church an eerie twilight blue.

The gust finally died down and the church was again silent for several moments. The priest stepped slowly towards Richard who remained concrete still. Just as he reached the corner of the altar an empty, tubular tone echoed around the rafters. It vibrated cobwebs from their century old hollows, startled dozens of bats and shook the very soul of the building. Still, Richard remained motionless.

Rather than fade, the lonely sound merely changed. It pitched in and out of audible range for some time but at last seemed to settle out into some kind of physical form. It was a slow moving mist which billowed out from above the altar, wisps reaching out to encircle both Richard and the priest. They explored and felt their presences before withdrawing in a slick motion accompanied by a sequence of low tones. They echoed among the relics and became apparent as distinct voices, wailing and bemoaning the fate of the eternally damned.

Suddenly a single voice became apparent among the drone. "Leave this place..." The voice was forceful but without aggression or malice. "Leave us."

All his life the priest had followed his faith with blind diligence and loyalty. But now, with all that he was witnessing he began to question whether he even believed what he had been preaching in the first place. He pushed the doubts to the back of his mind, trying to silence them with the story he had always been taught. As the voice spoke he stumbled back and made a short spurt for his sacristy, fumbling the poor box to the ground and slamming the door behind himself, locking it tight.

Richard eyes flicked open onto the altar and upon a much different world. The walls glowed as if the sun its self bore presence unto them. The air above the ground shimmered with a dark essence that now seemed to encompass the other worldly chapel. The candles that had shone so bright previously now burnt a quiet, almost black flame yet somehow still seemed to outline the solitary brass idols around them. A shivering atmosphere at Richards' feet grew in motion to mimic that of ocean mist rolling onto a dawn shore. It rose and encompassed the objects on the altar and eventually up to the pulpit. It moved as if attempting to prove all around it was insignificant when compared to its mere presence.

Suddenly the waves fell to the ground and broke on the stone slabs with no apparent reason or prompting. Still unphased, Richard began to move, casually reaching into an inner pocket and taking hold of a glass apothecary bottle. As he did, the darkness pressed up against his back, forcing him to pause his actions.

"Why are you here?" the voice of the darkness was whispered in an almost surreal way. "Why do you not listen?"

Richard let go of the bottle, allowing it to slip neatly back into his pocket and withdrew his hand down to his side. Turning around he found the shadows had manifested themselves into a figure. A young boy, no older than fourteen, his complexion pale and virtually translucent.

"How are you here?" it added, mystified by the mortal before him.

Richard took a breath, at a loss of what to say. Before he had a chance to even think, a second presence drifted across his path. From the back of the chapel it began to fade through the air, taller than the first, and started to take wavering steps towards Richard. It reached out and gently placed a hand on the boys shoulder, looking squarely at Richard as its features became discernible. Both looked as though they had once, long ago, worked on the fields, sowing and ploughing. Beyond that he dared not think about how the pair had come to be here. "You know why I'm here?" he asked the taller spirit.

The farmer moved in front of his son and without any kind of concern gazed straight at Richard. "Are you a God fearing man, sir?" he continued to silently stare ahead for a few more seconds. "How could you live with yourself? You don't know how long we've looked for a way back. You have no idea how desolate, how empty it is there. What reason have you got to send us back?"

"I do know..." Richard replied simply, pausing in thought for a moment, "...and I'm sorry...I truly am."

The farmer only now broke his gaze and stepped back in line with his son. "So am I."

The priest, shaking with disbelief, opened his eyes and unclasped his praying hands. He inched around and found the door handle, grasping it loosely at first, only tightening his grip as confidence returned to him. He re-opened the door onto an empty church hall, lacking any trace of what had happened. He stepped from the doorway and lightly trod towards the altar. He looked up towards the dark shrine, the candles now extinguished, and up at the brass cross that, even now, still glinted in the gloom. He looked around and realised the absence of the discarded poor box. Without even searching for it, he knew that the stranger had taken it. Although, with everything he had seen that night, for all the priest cared, he could keep it.

The house was at most 35, maybe 40 years old yet it had a strange presence about it, one that made it feel far older. It encompassed the rooms and flowed through its residents, becoming the buildings one defining feature. This sense of premature aging was only reinforced by the ornately decorated skirting boards, antique figurines and bookcases brimming with texts on spirituality and other worldly planes.

Richard placed the poor box, much more gently than it had become accustomed to over the course of the night, on a small shelf next to the door. Placing his keys alongside it, he slipped off his dripping jacket and dropped it over a cloak stand. No sooner as he had done that, from down the hall came the sound of the kitchen door swinging open and firm footsteps making their way up the polished wooden floor.

"Again?" came a young but raspy male voice belonging to the footsteps.

"It just seems such a waste," replied Richard, again placing a firm grasp on the poor box, this time only to toss it to his counterpart. "Take that round to Oxfam tomorrow, will you?"

"These charities…" he adjusted his grip on the box and held it to his side, "ninety percent of the money goes in the pocket of some fat cat."

"Mike, you see," he stepped forward and leant towards Michael, making him seem much shorter than he actually was, "it's better that at least some of the money, even if it *is* just ten percent, goes to who needs it rather than it all going in some cardinals wallet." He stood straight up again, where it became apparent that both men in fact had much the same build.

Michael breathed out heavily as Richard turned into the lounge but seemed to remember something as he moved to sit down. "Oh yeah, you got a call while you were out. It was Chris. He sounded pretty messed up."

"Tell me, when *isn't* he messed up?" he took at seat and leant on his knees. "Did he say why he phoned or was it just his general brand of assorted doomsday messages?"

"He said he wanted to meet you. Tonight, in the alley next to Queens Square take away at 12 o'clock," Michael moved to the other side of the room and leant on the hearth while Richard seemingly fell deep into thought. "You've not had a proper break in days now. Is it something to do with Halloween being in a few days?"

Richard jolted his head up and looked Michael straight in the eye. "How long now? Three years? How many times do I have to tell you? Halloween has no special bearing on anything, it's just a few dumb shits on the Other Side think they have a better chance of getting through. Believe me, they don't so it's not my problem."

"I just thought-"

"Nothing! Alright?" he sunk back into the seat and breathed deeply. "Now, Queens Square was it?"

"Yeah," Michael said cautiously, "the take away. I don't know what he wants."

There was silence for a few seconds as Richard contemplated the rest of the night. "I'd better check it out...You never know," he glanced at an ornate mahogany clock on the mantle piece. "Half nine, now," there was silence for another few seconds before he smoothly pushed up out of the chair and headed for the hallway.

"Rich, where you going?"

Richard grabbed his still dripping coat from the stand and slipped it on. "I need to stop off somewhere first," before anything more could be said he opened the front door and rushed out into the night.

"Hey!" Michael grabbed Richard's car keys from the shelf, "you forgot your keys!"

"I'll walk," came a voice from the rapidly shrinking silhouette.

"But it's still raining!"

There are not many people in this world who fully know what is going on. The purpose of life and other such related subjects. I never claimed to be one of them. I do take some pride in having a better idea than the majority of the populous, even if that idea is brought about by something I quiet often wished I didn't have.

I know there's more than one plane of existence, far more. The living world, that of the dead and a lonely, desolate plane known only as the Median World. Fringing on each side of the Median World bridging the planes of the living and the dead are border worlds. Places where lost souls manifest themselves and occasionally break through to appear as ghosts and poltergeists. Where most can only catch glimpses of these or witness their paranormal activities, I can see them as clear as day, as though they were actually there, even when they were not supposed to be. It's considered by some that my duty, the duty of all Medians, is to move them on to the next world, even if it is not their desire to go. There's no duty really, for me it's just about trying to keep a little sanity in the world.

By the time Richard had reached Gateshead Cemetery the rain had finally eased but still lingered in the air with a cold odiousness. He stood at the chest high iron fence of the graveyard and gazed in, scanning the grounds as though he were expecting to find something. Eventually his eyes focused onto a point just off an old chestnut tree, its branches swaying lethargically in the gentle breeze. As misty night air began to clear, it became apparent that there was the figure of a man. He seemed to be casually raking leaves, without a shudder or care for the bitterly cold air.

Richard turned away from the fence and made his way to the rusty gate. Gently pressing it open, the gate moaned from decades of disuse and finally screeched to a contented silence. The figure did not turn as he approached, apparently unaware of his presence. "Albert."

The figure continued to rake the leafless soil for a few more seconds before it began to speak in a deep, empty tone that was almost lost to the open air. "Have you finally come to do it then, son?" his rake occasionally caught a drifting leaf which crackled loudly against the soothing breeze. "I suppose my time is somewhat..." he looked up and leaned against his rake. His face was old and as empty as his words, dark and faded to an empty mist almost as if he belonged to the night, "overdue."

"You know I'm not here for that," he paused and tried to gain some idea of Albert's expression, or whether he, indeed, even had one. "I've had quite a busy week. You wouldn't happen to know anything about that, would you?"

He stood up straight and clasped the rake firmly in his hand. "One sees only what they wish to see..." casually he began to move towards Richard, in the process walking through an age old wheelbarrow that he had apparently been using at some point in time. "I wish only to see what it is my business to."

"I don't want to but I'll do it if I have to."

"Of course, what I wish and what I see are not always one in the same," he turned away and headed back towards the large tree he was working under, this time having the forethought to walk around the wheelbarrow. "Souls are restless, then again they always are, but especially now. You know why. But this is different...They're scared, and not just of moving on. There's something out there, something you don't want coming here," he placed the rake gently against the tree and turned back to Richard. "I've learnt a lot in my time here, most I didn't think was possible. But I am too old to worry about such things, now. That is the job of the young, your job," he took a step away from the rake and looked Richard straight in the eye. "Good luck Richard...And, please, take care of yourself." As his words drifted through the air his body began to fade into the night until all that was left was the eerie mist hovering above the graves.

Richard took a breath and looked down to the stone plaque at his feet:

HERE LIES:
ALBERT WEIGNRIGHT

BELOVED HUSBAND AND FATHER

1945-1988

WILL BE SORELY MISSED

"You too, dad," he turned and began to walk away from the grave as the rain started to fall again. He stopped at the rusted iron gate and looked back towards the large tree as it quickly became obscured by the night's mist. Turning quickly and once again flicking up his collar, he set off along the wet street.

For days the voices had haunted him, whispered omens in the back of his head, rumours of a dark shadow clouding everything just and good. Tonight was no different. With the quiet street it seemed as though the voices were screaming, and then there was the sudden realisation that they were. Richard was not the only one to hear them, though.

Chris wasn't someone many people liked, or even had anything much to do with. He had been diagnosed as mentally ill after several bouts of severe depression and from then onwards he had roamed homeless shelters with nowhere else to go, just another nameless face in the endless stream of human society. Appearances, it seemed, never told the full story for he was a Median, just like Richard.

After the death of his wife he had all but given up on life and did something no Median should ever do. He left himself open to the spirits wanting to cross back to the living world; a vessel for as many souls as it could bear.

The square was deadly quiet. The neon light of a take away flickered but cast virtually no light upon the puddle ridden concrete.

Richard glanced at his watch, shielding it from the driving rain. Twelve exactly.

"Rick? Is that you?" a voice tentatively came from the dark alleyway.

"Don't trust him!"

"I have to, he's our friend."

"You have to tell him what we've seen."

"Yes, only he can help."

"Be careful, Chris."

"I still say don't trust him!"

Richard strained to look into the dark from where the babbled confusion of statements had come. "Chris? Don't be afraid. It's Richard."

"What do you take us for? We are not afraid," Chris strode out into the dull light of the square and looked Richard up and down. He was filthy, unshaven and wore a trench coat that looked as though it belonged in a museum.

"Yes we are!" he recoiled back into the half darkness, his greasy and sodden blonde hair flicking over his face, "we are very afraid."

"Can I talk to Chris?" Richard asked as softly as he could, trying not to sound patronising.

Chris' head slowly emerged into the flickering neon light. "The world is changing, Rick. No-one's content on the Other Side-"

"As if they were in the first place," interrupted Chris to himself.

"-They can't do it, Rick, they can't..." he shook his head violently and began repeating his last two words over and over until he suddenly stopped and looked back up into the rain, "but if one could..."

Richard nodded shallowly. "Could what? Make it through to this side?" he breathed a sigh of frustration, it was clear this was not going to be easy. "What are you talking about, Chris?"

"The spirit can pass un-noticed but the physical can tip the balance," he stood up straight and looked Richard in the eye. "If he could...They all could..." Chris seemed to become transfixed by something and began watching the sky blankly, uncaring of the rain.

"He?" asked Richard irately. "Who? Who is He?!" his words flowed into the night and echoed in the ether. The whispered voices returned and scratched at the back of Richards head, it was garbled and chaotic but they whispered a word over and over again. A name.

Chris looked back to Richard and spoke a single word more clearly and coherently than he ever had before. "Millaian."

As he spoke the word, the chaotic whispers ceased, apparently content that they had finally been heard. Richard nodded shallowly and repeated the name with a dark sense of knowing. "Millaian."

II - A Dark Past

For now we see through a glass, darkly

-Corinthians 13:12

He used to be my friend. The only one I could tell about everything I saw, everything I knew. Then it happened. He became the a shadow of what he had been.

I hid the true nature of things from Michael for his own good...He shows great interest and, dare I say, promise but not yet the appreciation that the craft deserves. To know the truth would mean a risk beyond any that I am prepared to expose him to. One day he will want to know. One day he will need to know and on that day I will be there to give him the guidance he will surely need for what will lay ahead. For now, ignorance is a sweet bliss compared to the fate which may await yet him.

Richard pulled his finger roughly along the assorted volumes of spiritual encyclopaedia, through The Summoning texts and to a large, age old book. He tapped the tome violently with his index finger before ripping it from the bookcase and slamming it onto the coffee table. The decade old hardback was at least three inches thick and had its name embossed in gold leaf down the spine; 'The History of Old London'.

Richard wiped his still dripping fringe from his face and descended upon the book, pulling it open at an already marked page.

His gaze flowed down the yellowing page and eventually settled upon a small sepia picture of a stately looking family. The caption simply read 'The Millaians.'

"You," whispered Richard to himself as he settled his finger over a specific figure in the centre of the photo. The figure stood tall and stern over the rest of the family, almost as though he had some sort of menace about him. The finger slid from the picture to a name just to the side and a short paragraph below it.

Joseph Millaian

Respected among his peers and feared by the workers in his factories, Joseph was the third generation of industry owning Millaians to come to London. He owned lucrative properties in Manchester and Liverpool, topping off his enterprise with his purchase in 1884 of a textile facility in the centre of Birmingham. Reaching London in 1886, Joseph failed in an attempted bid to take over Thomas & Co. in the countries capital. Later that year he was reported missing, only to be declared dead by suicide, presumably from the immense stress of business. Yet to this day his body has never been recovered and it is unknown what truly happened to him.

Richard slowly stood back up, continuing to stare at the text, gritting his teeth with deep thought.

"Rich?" came a voice from the doorway.

He swung round, slamming the book closed as his did and settled his gaze towards Michael. "It's a little late for you isn't it?"

"I could say the same for you," he looked him up and down. "You're dripping wet."

"I realise that," he leant flat palmed on the book as Michael began to move into the room. "Chris was…He was his usual self."

"Always is," he craned his head around Richard to look at the book. "What're you reading?"

"Nothing!" Richard snapped quickly, "…Just…Some family history."

"Alright, well-" he stood straight again and began to move back towards the door, "I'll see you tomorrow then."

Richard nodded and waited until Michael was completely gone before releasing his grip on the book. He gazed at it again and sighed heavily. "What's the connection?" He again sighed heavily and replaced the text to its appointed position.

As he retracted his hand, he glanced at the clock in the centre of the mantle and then slumped down into his armchair.

1:37am. It wasn't like those things in the night were anything new to Richard, far from it. Still, each second closer to the darkness he came, the more his concern grew. He never liked to sleep at this time of year, no-one in his position would, but then no-one is impervious to the will of their body, either.

As he sat, the whispers scratched at the back of his mind, repeating that same name over and over. Soon, though, their drone became but white noise and he began to sink into the dark sleep which forever left him vulnerable and consumed with fear.

"The night shall come…"

And so it did.

The dreams which dwelt within were filled with the shadows of untold figures. There was a numbing silence which pierced the very soul its self and the brightest light in the darkest of places. Then there were those stood before it, each wanting a vessel as much as the next, so close yet just out of reach. Behind them stood a man, seemingly possessing no desire for a vessel or to return to the mortal plane.

Richard stepped towards the man with the gathered shadows around him parting like water. He reached forward for his shoulder but before he could grasp him, the figure turned and looked up sombrely.

"Chris?"

Sunlight washed in all about him and dissolved the darkness as quickly as it had manifested its self. Richard flinched and squinted his eyes as it became apparent that he was back in his own world.

"What happened last night?" Michael's voice came from the dazzling black.

Richard cracked opened his eyes, barely managing to focus on him. "Last night?" he rolled his eyes over to the clock that he was certain he had only looked at moments ago. "Nine thirty?" he groaned and shook his head while growing more accustomed to the light.

"With Chris..." Michael took a deep breath. "I heard on the radio this morning...He's-"

"-Dead," he leant forward and cradled his head in his hands. "Don't ask me how I know."

He looked cautiously to Richard and began again. "He was found just outside Queens Square...They didn't say how he died," Michaels mind swelled with possibilities and finally one slipped out. "You didn't-?" his almost comment was met with quite possibly the sharpest gaze he'd ever experienced. "No, no...Of course you didn't," he looked away and spoke in tones he didn't intend to be heard. "It's just what with his condition...It would have been a release-"

"Listen!" Richard pushed himself from the chair, pulling himself upright, without even wavering. "Christopher was always my friend...He still is-" he breathed sombrely, "wherever he is." He relaxed slightly and rushed past Michael towards the staircase. There was no particular urgency but his step was one that was not to be stopped.

Michael watched Richard move swiftly up the stairs before turning away and whispering simply, "These things happen."

But they don't. Not like this. Something was wrong.

I could have stopped it. I was the last to see him. I am his last true friend, a lot of good that did him. In the end I abandoned him just like everyone else. For all the good I did I might as well have killed him myself...It couldn't have just been a coincidence, he knew something he wasn't supposed to and now so did I. The more I thought about it the more I knew it was better to keep Michael in the dark. I still wasn't sure how safe that would keep him though. Kids like that...They draw attention...

Richard casually opened his bedroom door and let it drift gently shut as he passed through. The room was much like the rest of the house; rustic beyond its time and filled with bookcases stocked with assorted volumes on the afterlife.

Across from the foot of his bed was an oak desk littered with various scribbled scraps of paper and a single large, half burnt candle centred at the back of it. Around it stood an arrangement of small statuettes and precious looking rocks, each presumably with a significance all of their own.

He took a silver flick lighter from his inside pocket and lit the large candle before laying heavily down on the bed and flicking the lighter closed with a snap. Slowly his eyes drifted shut, compelled to close by the darkness of the room. The only thing that allowed him to cling onto the waking world was a small beam of dusty light which managed to find a gap between the still drawn curtains. In the murky darkness the air changed.

"Hello Rich," a voice said soothingly.

Richard lifted his eyelids gently, looking towards the desk and the lit candle. It still burned but now darkly, giving off no light, only an electrical blue aurora backed by an eerie black, absent of movement and warmth. He fully opened his eyes and peered carefully around the now grey and lifeless feeling room. His eyes settled on a shape standing against that lone beam of sunlight and without them even adjusting to the unusual brightness, he knew who he was looking at.

"You called...How could I refuse?" came the voice again, the figure stepping closer to Richards's bed and into a better light. He was now neat and tidy, with a sense of self unlike any he'd had in such a long time. "I'm free now."

"So it was you..." Richard sat up and turned, pushing himself up on the side of the bed. "Chris, I can save you...Bring you back-"

"No! I thought we had an agreement," Chris looked Richard in the eye, "I'm too close to her now...I can't leave."

"It could take years to find her."

"Fine, then, she's more than worth it," his voice was filled with love and joy at the thought of reuniting with his wife. "It's better for him as well. For the future…How is the boy, anyway? I take it you haven't told him yet?"

Richard shook his head with conviction. "No, he's just not ready for it. Maybe when he's more like his old man," he raised an eyebrow towards Chris. "Who else could pull me into the border world but you?"

"Listen, Rich, I wouldn't have done it if I had a choice but things are not exactly wonderful on this side. That name…It's not even the half of it," he breathed deeply. "I've brought you here to warn you. It's far worse than I thought," he suddenly became agitated and looked around as if someone was searching for him. "The night is coming, Rich. Everlasting night, like nothing we've ever seen before-"

He placed a hand firmly on Chris's shoulder to steady him and spoke harshly. "Chris! Who was it? Who killed you?"

"Not who-" he again looked deeply into Richards eyes, "…I can't tell you much but believe nothing. All I know is that he is the tide…He brings the wave…"

"Who? Who!?" Richard shook him as he began to look around again, terror filling his eyes. "Millaian?"

"How do you know that name?" he gazed, stunned, at Richard for a second before something snatched away his attention. "He's here." Chris began to back into a corner, cowering from something apparently coming from the opposite wall. A thing Richard could not see, as much as he tried. Suddenly the blue candle began dancing and the curtains twitched violently.

The papers on Richards desk blew up and started flying around the room as a deafening hiss filled his ears, forcing him to cover them and fall to his knees. He looked up at Chris, who had backed up against the wall and was continually mouthing a single word. Finally his words overpowered the din enough for Richard to briefly hear. "Lancer!"

He knew this word. It was a name, one he knew well. Before his mind could comprehend what was taking place, a burst of dust shot from the wall Chris had been intently staring at. Finally Richard could see what he had been so afraid of. From it materialised a tall man who reached down towards Richards friend with a thin, almost bone like hand.

"I am your master now!" it stated in a raspy, commanding voice. It was about to grasp Chris' face when it suddenly turned towards Richard, a cloak of black sweeping behind it. He backed up against the bed as it began to approach. Its whole body was as thin as its hand, its face longer than any he had ever seen. It's eye sockets were sunken far into its skull and wrinkled, grey features were seemingly set directly onto the bone it's self. It began to speak again as it now reached for Richard. "I am the master of all!"

As the hand fell towards him, he backed as far into the bed sheets as he could and, closing his eyes, screamed at the top of his lungs.

Then all was again silent. He gradually opened his eyes, breathing shallow and quick, still in sheer terror. Slowly coming back to his senses, he heard heavy footsteps beating up the stairs and finally the door burst open with a clatter.

"Rich! What happened?" asked Michael, moving around the room only to be met with a quick nod between the rapid breathing. "I just heard a thud and then you scream," he helped Richard up onto the bed and sat down next to him. "Are you alright?"

He breathed out slowly, regaining his composure and looked to the corner where Chris had been cowering. "I don't know."

"It's alright now, you're safe," Michael thought about the statement for a moment, knowing full well that Richard would never be this disturbed over nothing. Whatever had done this must be truly awful and wasn't about to just go away. It occurred to him that it might not be just Richard who was in danger. "I'll go and put the kettle on," he stood up and began to walk towards the door but stopped just short.

"Michael…" Richard pushed himself to his feet once more and wavered slightly before facing the door. "There are some things you should know," he thought about telling him everything, all the things he had tried to protect him from for so long. The truth of his past. A truth that could bring down the darkness. After what had just happened he came close to telling him. He at least needed to know what was going on, Richard thought, for his own safety. He deserved that much at least. "I'm not even completely sure what, though…I think we should find out together."

Michael had become accustomed to how cryptic Richard could be and had learnt that it would all become apparent in time, so with that notion in mind he simply nodded, saying nothing.

"Get the car keys, we're going to the library."

If not for the drone of the engine, the car would have been silent. Richard had been moved by his recent ordeals and it preyed ever more upon his mind that Michael should know the truth about his farther. He didn't know why, something just told him that the time was close. He idly slid his hands around the wheel and gripped it tight, deep in thought, barely concentrating on the road.

"What happened?" Michael had suddenly turned and was gazing at Richard timidly. "When you called out?"

Richard blinked and tightened his grip on the wheel again. That face had been embossed on his mind, the skeletal, horrifying malice in flesh. It had been clear for a long time that Michael knew what Richard was. He knew all about his work but he was never told any of the details, kept safe for all these years from the knowledge of a Medians true nature. His own true nature or at least what he would eventually become. The thought of telling him had consumed Richard for the longest time but, especially now with the memory of that spectre, he had decided he shouldn't. He couldn't.

"Nothing...", he replied at last, weakly. "I just had an uncooperative client, that's all."

Michael was about to question the reply but his tongue was held by a common sense he sometimes wished he didn't have.

"We're here," Richard stated flatly, pulling into the car park of a large, three storey building. As he got out, he looked over the roof of the car and stared at Michael blankly. "Don't concern yourself with this or it'll concern its self with you."

Michael nodded without much conviction and made his way into the library. He was unsure whether he had said something wrong or if Richard's attitude was simply for his own good. Lord knows he had known it both ways.

"Ahh, Richard!" an attendant called, waving him over. "Haven't seen you in here for quite the long while," he took Richards hand, shaking it firmly, promptly moving on to Michael, "and is this the lad you've told me so much about?"

Richard croaked and swallowed awkwardly. "Yes…"

"I haven't the foggiest why you've never brought him in before. He reminds me of my lad," the elderly attendant seemed to reminisce from seeing Michael, momentarily drifting off. "Got kids of his own now, he has."

Richard smiled half heartedly. "Well, we're here to do some nineteenth century research. On a particular individual, in fact," he breathed heavily. "Joseph Millaian."

The attendant squinted and scratched his balding head. "Millaian, you say? Name sounds familiar but for the life of me I don't know where from," he thought some more before cheerfully looking up again and turning to his computer. "Oh well, it'll come back to me. For now we'll just have to look him up, shall we?" he briefly glanced at Richard again with a large grin across his face. "Wonderful things these computers, all I do is type in the name here, see?" he pressed each button with a single finger and waited for a second. "Ahh, there we go. It gives you a list of all the books he would've been in," he printed a copy of the reading list and handed it to Richard who nodded and smiled again.

The list had four primary titles, all local history books, with a number of censuses and other miscellaneous documents listed beneath. At the very bottom, marked in red as checked out, was a single title; 'Vessel' by Christophe Guillaume. It had a much later date of publication than its counterparts and was not a local history text but was simply categorized under non-fiction. Richard folded the slip of paper and slid it neatly into a side pocket before turning to Michael. "Well, we'd better get looking then."

No matter how he felt, books always managed to brighten Richards's mood, even if just for a while. It was partly why almost every wall of his house was lined with volume after volume of them. Of course, they were the only thing that had ever really comforted him as a child. Retreating into a world of words and dreams kept the voices away and the world from driving him to them.

The hours passed slowly, every one becoming more tiresome than the last. As they did, each of the four texts found themselves open on a narrow plywood table. Richard gazed over them intently leaving Michael to idly flick through the pages as each was tossed aside. For all their effort there was nothing more than the life and achievements of a simple Victorian entrepreneur. There was barely even anything on his disappearance although this, in itself, did seem to intrigue Richard more than anything else of the man's life.

He pushed back from the table and arched his back, realising how long he had been lent over the book. "This is useless."

"What are we actually looking for?" asked Michael, looking up from a page. "We've been at this for ages and you've still got me in the dark."

"Anything..." he rubbed his face and run his hands through his hair with a sigh, "anything at all." As he spoke the attendant emerged from behind a pillar, grasping a small, scruffy looking notebook. He shuffled over to the table, prompting Michael to check his watch.

"I remembered," he exclaimed happily, waving a free finger loosely. "I was sure I'd heard that name before so I went searching in the achieves and found this," he produced the notebook and handed it to Richard. "I'm not sure what it is, it's been down there for decades, I think. I can't read French but that name just stuck in my head, you know."

Richard picked through the pages gently, flicking past paragraphs of hand written text and strange diagrams before slamming it shut in one hand and staring at the cover. It had a single word scrawled across it 'Navire.'

"French..." Richard reached into his pocket and pulled out the slip of paper. Unfolding it, he looked at the single absent book and then pointed it out to the attendant. "Do you remember who took this out?"

"I think so..." he thought for a second. "Yes...Now I remember. He didn't have a membership, just took it out on short loan. Small man he was, about the same age as you," he waved his finger at Richard once again. "Untidy looking sort, though, very unsure of himself...Oh and that trench coat-"

Richard looked up quickly. "It wasn't him," he mumbled after a few seconds, "he didn't know I already knew that name," he turned to Michael abruptly, his eyes widening. "Navire…"

"Vessel," finished Michael, pleased he might have finally found a use for that French A-Level.

The attendant looked between the two of them and stepped back slightly. "I think you should take that…" he glanced cautiously at the notebook, "you'll probably understand it a lot better than me."

Richard looked back to the notebook and gripped the leather cover tightly as Michael thanked the attendant. After a moment he loosened his grip and run a hand softly across it. "It was him," he spoke quietly and acted as if he'd much rather be somewhere else, "in my trance. It was this…Millaian. He's not what these books say he was," he tapped the closest open book firmly with the notebook before withdrawing it close to him, "not anymore. He's changed, corrupted somehow. But it's like nothing I've ever heard of."

"You said it wasn't him," Michael ventured. "Who wasn't?"

Richard exhaled heavily, finally conceding that there were some things he couldn't keep to himself. "Chris. When I went to see him last night he told me about Millaian but…" he wasn't sure how to say it but tried to choke the words out regardless. "It wasn't Chris. I did see him in my trance, though…right before that bastard took him," he clenched his free fist, "this Millaian guy. But Chris… he was like I remembered him. He's not always been like you knew him. Once he was my best friend…" His fist unclenched and a small smile creped onto his lips but was quickly wiped away once he realised he was straying off topic. "He warned me about Millaian again and was surprised when I already knew the name. Michael, I think he's been in the border world for days already."

"How is that-?" he paused for a second. "Possession? Maybe Chris wasn't in there at all. He had multiple personalities, after all. Maybe he could have been dead for days and it was just the spirits inhabiting his body all along," he glanced at the book. "A vessel."

The smile returned to Richards's lips as he began to wonder why he had never let Michael in on his work before. "You're smart, kid, I'll give you that," he slipped the notebook into one of his many concealed pockets and was about to head to the door but abruptly turned back to Michael instead. "What's the next move, then?"

He thought and cautiously twitched his mouth, debating whether his idea was right. "Try and get to see the body? That could tell us a lot, I guess?"

Richard smiled once more. "Very smart."

III - VI of I

Forsake not an old friend; for the new is not comparable to him

-Ecclesiasticus 9:10

A lifeless body wasn't something I particularly took pleasure in seeing usually but the thought of his like that turned my stomach in a different way. Then again, given how things had turned out I suppose I already had. I'll never understand why I hadn't seen it. Maybe I just didn't want to but his body was empty already when I had met him that night. Without the original soul the host will die within a matter of days, no matter how many parasites try to maintain it. There was something more, though, Chris was a bigger part of all of this than I thought and seeing him one more time may be the only way to know how. Getting in to see him, on the other hand, could prove to be more than a little testing.

The day was getting late. Dusk was already beginning to create a haze over the horizon causing and the low hanging sun to become orange in the sky.

Richard walked slowly to the hospital entrance and looked up at the building, shaking his head, then looked to Michael who followed at a distance.

"People die here..." he took a step back away from the hospital, "not good for me."

"You can feel them, can't you? Everyone who's crossing over in there?" said Michael raising his voice as Richard moved ever farther away.

Richard placed a hand firmly on the glass pane of a swing door and pushed it open harshly. "Yes." He followed the wide swing with a wide stride into a place where nothing was real to him.

The recently dead roamed the building, waiting for their time to move on, filling the silence of life with the chorus of death. It was subtle but near unbearable to those who could hear it.

"Getting to see him won't be a piece of cake, you do realise?" he stopped in the almost completely empty waiting room.

There was a receptionist sat behind a waist high desk, slowly punching at her keyboard and a lone man waiting quietly, presumably for an appointment.

Michael hurried through the doors, trying to draw as little attention to himself as possible. "Can't you just go into your trance thing and go in without anyone seeing you?" he whispered loudly.

"No," Richard snapped, "my body still has a physical presence in this world. It's not like it makes me invisible or anything," he tried not to sound patronising but didn't succeed. "Anyway, I'm not about to do that in here even if it did. They'd tear me apart."

Richard turned and began to walk towards a set of doors leading into the main hospital. As he did, he shot Michael a dark scowl, pressing home just how dangerous this could be for him. Even so, some part of him was pleased with how scared Michael looked with such little effort. At least now he might take the whole situation a little more seriously.

Richard had just about reached the doors when the receptionist jumped up from her chair and leaned over the desk.

"Sir, I'm afraid visiting hours end at 5 O'Clock and we request that last entries are at four thirty," she hung over the desk for several more seconds until Richard backed away from the door at which point she returned to her seat and resumed typing.

"Well that didn't work," Richard stated casually, walking back to Michael again.

"Really?" he replied sarcastically, "and there's me thinking they'd let you just waltz in."

Richard manoeuvred behind the rows of seats, making sure he was out of the receptionist's sight, and set about inspecting a wall mounted fire alarm.

"What are you doing?" Michael loudly whispered again, this time briefly drawing the attention of the single waiting patient.

"Just looking," he pulled the sleeve of his jacket across a clenched hand and quickly hit the alarm, breaking the glass and almost immediately setting off a loud buzzer.

The receptionist looked up abruptly and scanned across the room before hurrying through the door behind the desk.

"Problem solved, no-one will bother us now."

Michael looked around as Richard set off towards the doors again. "I can't believe you just did that! Do you know how much trouble you've just caused them?"

"Relax," Richard said turning back for a moment, "they'll realise it's a false alarm in a few minutes and everything will be fine." He wondered briefly whether it would actually be that simple but decided that it wasn't worth thinking about. "Now come on, it's given us just enough time to get into the morgue."

"This isn't even a good plan," Michael mumbled, looking around in a panic one last time before rushing into the main hospital after Richard.

With the alarm blazing, assorted staff hurried around trying to find out what was happening whilst doctors fussed over their patients safety. In the confusion the two interlopers were as good as invisible, slipping through the bustling corridors without so much as a second glace.

They arrived at the Morgue and slipped in just as the alarm ceased, causing Richard to look up and around.

"Damnit, thought it'd keep them busy a bit longer than that," he swung round, taking in the room as he did. "We need to hurry."

There were a number of stainless steel tables, bodies led neatly on each with thin linen blankets draped across them. To the side of the room, under a large hanging light, was another table. This one with rolling tables scattered around it, filled with assorted medical tools.

Michael took a step forward to inspect closer, only to find that the table had another body led on it, this one already having been victim to the mercy of the pathologist.

"It's not Chris is it?" asked Richard, making Michael start backwards in fright.

He took a shallow breath, realising how foul the air was as he did. "No...No, I don't think so," he shuddered and moved away from the autopsy, taking up a position next to the door as Richard started towards the covered bodies. "How come we found this place so fast, it's almost as though you knew where you were going."

Richard took hold of the sheet on the first table tentatively then threw it back, only to sigh when he found it was not Chris and move on to the next one. "Let's just say this isn't my first visit here," he grabbed hold of the second cover, more confidently this time, and again threw it back but was driven back by an invisible force, knocking the breath out of him.

After composing himself his gaze followed something across the room for a few seconds and then through the back wall. He shook his head and gritted his teeth. "Inconsiderate bastard," he quickly moved on to the next corpse, this time pulling the sheet off while keeping a distance. He peered at the body and smirked slightly. "Bingo!"

"You've found him?" Michael stepped up and examined the body. It was Chris alright. Unwashed, unshaven and still damp from the previous night. What colour that had been in his already pale complexion had now been sapped from his body, leaving only an empty grey husk.

"They've taken his coat," Richard stated suddenly, "check in the draws," he threw his arm back and pointed at a steel wall cabinet with several roller draws in its lower section. "He might've left something in the pockets," as he spoke he inspected and searched the body, finding nothing but dirt and linen.

Michael opened the top draw and pulled out a long, stained trench coat which unfurled to full length as he held it and hung heavily to the ground. "Is this it?" he padded the pockets tentatively and removed a folded note from one of the side pockets.

"What did you find?" Richard took the piece of paper and flicked it open. The note was damp and the writing scrawled, the smeared ink barely legible against the wet paper. He read it and sighed deeply, gazing at the words sorely. "I'm sorry my friend," he laid a hand on the corpses arm for a moment and then took the note with both hands. "The end is coming," he dictated, "they are all gone, except one. A powerful spirit who promises me release, promises me her. I don't believe him but I can't resist, I'm too weak. I hear him, hear his schemes. 'Seven of one and I shall be born again' he tells me. I am the one."

"What does it mean?" asked Michael. "Seven of one and I shall be born again?"

"Honestly, I don't know," he folded the note again and reached into his pocket, pulling out the strange book, "but it's got to have something to do with this," he waved the book loosely and leant against the table, placing it down.

"Richard," Michael said slowly, stepping backwards as his eyes widened. "It's moving," he pointed to Chris' arm as it raised, the fist clenching as it went.

Richard bolted upright and drew his gun, swinging around. The grey body sat up and looked around, examining the room and settled on the book Richard had left at the end of the table. "This has never happened before," he told himself, unsure whether to think any of this was real or not.

"The text has awoken me," the corpse said in an unsettlingly deep, grating voice while reaching for the book, "it has been too long."

Richard shuddered at his best friend being used like some puppet. "Freeze right there!" he shouted, pushing the gun forward as the zombie gripped the book, its dead hands seemly able to move independently of the rest of its being. "Just what the hell are you?"

"Richard Weignright. I should thank you for awaking me. I also appreciate you returning my text," it held up the book, grinning on half of its face. "But it is somewhat earlier than I had hoped."

"I said who are you?" he thought for a second and grimaced, "and how do you know who I am?"

"I know you, Rich…" it readjusted its wrist with a sharp snap, "I know everything this host knew," it peered back at Michael and saw fear wash across Richards face. Slowly it's grin grew wider. "Does that concern you, my friend? And, oh yes, you know me. For a moment I had you within my grasp. Someone of your...talents... could be very useful to me but, alas, you slipped away."

"You can't be," he backed away slightly, putting up a free arm to try and protect Michael, "you were who he was talking about in that note. That's why you were after him in the border world."

"Yes. Control the mind, control the body. And as for that note, I really did try to stop him but his will was a great deal stronger than I had anticipated. Admirable, to be sure, but I still had to dispose of him, regardless."

"Son of a bitch!" Richard growled, "You killed my best friend!"

"Indeed," the embodiment of Millaian turned on the table and slid from it, grasping the notebook tightly, "I must thank you again, but just like your friend, I no longer have need for you." With slow, deliberate movements he removed a scalpel from a nearby tray.

"I said don't move!" he pushed the gun as far forward as he could while trying to back away from the psychopathic corpse. "I'm warning you!"

"Come now, we both know that it is empty," his words were calm and gentle as he started to move forward, knife in hand.

"Good point," Richard breathed quickly, lowering the weapon. "But this isn't!" he spun around, reaching into his coat with his free hand and pulled a vial from his inside pocket. In a single, smooth movement he popped the cork and threw the liquid at Millaian.

The substance splashed onto his face, immediately burning deeply into the tissue and, with a loud hiss, made him drop to his knees, screaming in agony.

Richard hustled Michael out of the door, running through corridors and crowds of bewildered medics until they arrived outside. By this time the sun was as good as down and twilight had firmly set in.

"That's it!" coughed Richard, gasping for breath. "We're getting to the bottom of this!" he growled, storming towards the car.

"What was that stuff you threw at him?" asked Michael, still cringing from what he had just seen.

"A mixture of extracts and oils. I normally use it to send spirits back to their rightful plane if they don't cooperate. Perfectly harmless to mortals," he paused for a moment in thought. "I'm just glad I didn't use it last night, it was my last bottle," he gave a slight chuckle amidst the anger and grasped the handle of the car door.

"How did you know it would work on him, then?" Michael already regretted asking the question, fearing the answer would be 'I didn't'.

"Best guess," he replied, shrugging slightly, "I figured he wasn't mortal anymore so something had to happen."

Michael rolled his eyes and leant on the roof of the car. "So where now then?"

"Chris' place, it's the only option. I did some-" he took a deep breath in, "-things for him there."

Michael looked suspiciously at him but eventually nodded, still trying to recover his composure. "Fine then, let's go," he rubbed his face and pushed his hair from his eyes. "I think I'm better off not asking any questions right now."

Richard nodded, "good choice."

Millaian, still on his knees, cradled his hosts face. Pulling his hands away, he could see that seared, melted flesh now covered them and thick, dark blood began to drip between his fingers, pooling on the ground. He shook with a tormented combination of pain and rage and clenched his fists tightly, each bone in them cracking in succession.

Two doctors burst through the door only to be abruptly stopped in their tracks. "What on Earth happened here?" one asked, looking around the room while the second stared at the knelt body.

"I live," came Millaians voice from the ground. As it did, he began to straighten up, unclenching his hands and reaching down to recover the notebook and scalpel.

"Get security," the second doctor whispered to the first, making him rush off again. "Don't worry; everything's going to be alright."

"No, it won't..." he turned his head and in the light the doctor saw his true appearance.

Nearly all of the skin on his face was missing and what remained was disfigured and burnt beyond recognition. His eyes bulged from their sockets and swivelled precariously on the bone. The holes in his face, covered only by a few surviving tendons, seeped a brown puss, the fetid coagulant of liquidised flesh and post mortem blood. He smiled a lipless grin and got to his feet.

"At least, not for you." Millaian lunged forward, forcing the razor sharp blade forwards towards the doctor. A single, stifled scream rang out through the corridors and then there was silence once more.

I must have been crazy. Michael may have been scared but he just couldn't resist asking the questions he said he wouldn't. Questions I daren't answer but ones I couldn't just leave hanging.

He wanted to know about me and Chris, our history. That alone I may have been able to deal with but then he starting asking about how a guy like Chris could hold down a flat. The truth was that I was the one who paid the rent. I had done so for all these long years and that wasn't something I could just explain away. I simply tried to avoid his questions and said barely enough to make sure he didn't think I was ignoring him.

What had happened tonight was almost incomprehensible to me. If it had been enough to knock me this much off balance then I can't even begin to imagine the impact it had on Michael. I wanted him out, away from all of this but it wasn't safe for him anymore. Millaian had made that much clear.

I needed answers and Chris was the only one who could give them to me. By the time we got to his place, though, I realised we were in for much more than I had bargained for.

Across Chris' door were various scores and marks, each tinted with a different colour, as though the wood had been treated in some way.

"Protection," Richard stated abruptly, reaching into a pocket for his bundle of keys. "The things I said I did for him," he waved his hand over the markings, "simple incantations and oils in the wood. Trickery basically, but they made him feel better. Something slightly more powerful inside, though," he spoke with particular self satisfaction about his work. He found the key and slid it into the lock, opening the door with the ease of a person who did it regularly. "And don't ask me why I have a key."

Michael put his hands up defensively and just let Richard talk, starting to understand that even if he get the answers he sought, he probably wouldn't like them.

He stepped in line with Richard as he passed over the threshold, noticing a trail of salt along the carpet just inside the doorway. "So, this more powerful thing?"

Richard moved into the living area and pointed to a table in the corner with a large section of amethyst perched centrally on it.

"Amethyst?" Michael said, clearly unimpressed. "Is that it? A nice table decoration?"

"Table decoration?" he snapped, turning harshly. "Do you realise how much those things cost?"

Michael placed his hands on his hips and stared at Richard. "A bloody lot I should think. They're rip offs, its probably not even real quartz!"

"Look, it *is* real and if the people selling it knew just what it could do then it'd cost a whole lot more," he calmed down and breathed slowly. "It's a prison, of sorts. You could say it's naturally tuned to the wavelength of bad spirits, those who would want to inflict hurt on someone, especially someone in Chris' state, and it captures them," he looked back at Michael whose cyes had glazed over. He watched him for a few seconds longer before shaking his head and walking off into Chris's bedroom. "Forget it."

For a moment more Michael looked at the half geode in front of him, thinking about what Richard had said and took it upon himself to try and sound as though he actually understood any of it. "Yeah, well, I know what you mean. It's just that you can't be too carful these days. Everyone's trying to rip someone off," he began to move towards the bedroom when Richards voice echoed loudly along the hall.

"Don't come in here, boy!" The door was slammed shut and a thud followed, almost like someone had fallen heavily against it.

Michael moved slowly along the hall, looking at the door with suspicion. "What's wrong? You're scaring me," he reached the door and moved a hand towards the knob but hurriedly withdrew it, instead tilting his head and placing an ear against the wood. As far as he could tell, the room was deathly silent, broken only by the throbbing of his uneasy heart. "Rich?" he finally breathed, pulling his head away from the door and looking around the hall.

Michael cocked his head and peered at the slightly ajar door of the bathroom at the end of the hall. Beginning to move again, he continued to gaze at the door with a growing sense that something wasn't right. Through the crack he could see that there were dark red flecks across the floor. Tentatively he reached a shaking hand forward and gently pressed against the door, leaning in as it slowly swung open to reveal smeared red streaks leading towards a large pool of drying blood standing out brightly against the white tiles. He held his breath, looking up and around the room at whitewashed walls coated in layer upon layer of blood, sprayed around in a manner almost beyond believability.

Eventually he was forced to breath and as he did the putrid stench hit his nostrils, making him gag and cover his mouth with his sleeve. Panning around the horrific scene, he laid eyes on the worst of it all. In the bath lay the contorted body of a young man, his throat slit deep and his limbs bent in ways that were not naturally possible. He was wearing what looked like a suit, now stained beyond recognition with his own blood.

"He tried to escape," a voice came from behind Michael, startling him into swinging around. "The others didn't even make that far." Richard spoke in low tones, his voice quivering and his eyes becoming redder with every passing moment.

He'd never seen anything like this. He never thought he would or at least hoped beyond any reasonable hope that he never would. It was little wonder, then, when a tear finally broke from the corner of his eye and ran slowly down his cheek.

"Others?" Michael breathed, horrified at the idea that there may be more in this state.

Richard nodded, making Michael to shudder violently. "Five more, all like him," he flicked his eye vaguely to the bathtub. "I can't let you stay here-"

"I don't want to be," Michael cut Richard off abruptly, barging past him and rushing outside.

"Alright," Richard whispered to himself as he heard the front door slam shut.

He turned back to the bedroom and cautiously approaching it again, preparing himself for the presence of at least one of the departed. Although he had been in the house for a while now and really should have felt something. There should have been a remaining spirit, even the after-presence of one but there was nothing there but that horrific stench, filling every breath with decay.

He pressed against the door which dragged against the thick bedroom carpet as it opened. Inside was humid and dark with the curtains completely drawn, forcing Richards eyes to adjust to the gloom. As they did several shapes on the ground came into focus. The shapes slowly gained structure and soon faces. Five more bodies were strewn about the ground, the carpet around them saturated with their blood, still fresh in some places. He closed his eyes for a moment, taking as deep a breath as he could without vomiting, before re-entering that wretched room.

Stepping over the bodies and treading lightly on the stained carpet, he made his way to a dresser in front of the darkened window, covered in scribbled notes and harbouring an assortment of books. They were spiritual texts, similar to those lining the walls of Richard's house, only these were bloodied and battered. Similarly, the dressers mirror had been subjected to much the same fate with large cracks running its entire length and parts of it shattered entirely. Blood had also been spurted across its surface with the spatter making a clear reflection impossible to make out.

Around it were seven small pictures. They were of the victims now lifelessly sprawled around the room. Each had a thick black marker line across it, bar a single image of a woman on the right hand side of the mirror. She looked near her thirties and had shoulder length, chestnut hair falling evenly around her face. Richard was caught for a second by her eyes, a strange dark blue that sparkled in a way he recognised. She wasn't like the others, he knew that much.

Looking around at the bodies he confirmed that she had not suffered the same fate as the others, at least not yet, and stared again at the picture. Beneath it, scrawled across the mirror in the same black marker that struck out the images and partially obscured by the dried blood spray, was a name; 'Hollie'.

Richard mouthed the name and abruptly began rooting through the assortment of notes on the dresser, no longer caring about the blood that was being smeared across his hands. Finally he stopped and slowly lifted a small local newspaper cutting to what small amount of light there was.

The scrap mentioned one Hollie Michelle Reade, twenty seven years of age, who had been rushed into hospital with a suspected drug overdose nearly a week ago only to pass away two days later.

Richard sighed and hung his head, tossing the slip of paper back onto the pile of scraps. His hand, as it began to fall back to his side, was suddenly diverted and grasped a thin book half emerging from the heap of paper. He carelessly removed the test, pulling the majority of the scraps onto the floor, and squinted at the cover. It had a renaissance style portrait depicting the devils temptation of Adam and Eve in The Garden of Eden and above it in large, red, gothic letters read the title: 'VESSEL – Adapted by Christophe Guillaume'.

Richard swallowed heavily as he began to flick through the book, a chill creeping down his spine. Much of it contained the same drawings as Millaians notebook, only much neater and in English. Flipping through a few more pages, he found one that had been marked and amongst the text a sentence highlighted. As he read, a cold dread filled his body and he began to shake.

'VI of I and I shall live : VII of I and I shall be born again'

Everything suddenly fell into place. Chris had been coerced in some way to kill those people and consume their essence so that the parasite inside him could take control of a new host.

Richard had never known anything like it. There had been myths of such things but never had it really happened. It was becoming clearer now that he knew what VI of I meant. Millaian still needed this Hollie for something although he dreaded knowing what it would be. Still, she was dead now, had been for a good few days, more than enough time to cross over…Unless…And then it hit him.

That sparkle in her eyes. She wasn't just anyone, she had a power that none of the others had, a power Millaian needed, and someone like that never goes quietly to the Other Side.

Richard knew exactly where he could find her, that much was easy enough to deduce. Getting to her, on the other hand, would be a challenge all to its self for she was in the Desert of Desolation its self. The Median World.

He slammed shut the book, cursing softly to himself, and slid it clumsily into a side pocket of his jacket. Looking back at the picture of Hollie, he quickly ripped from the mirror before rushing out the room and into the fresh night air. Taking a deep breath to clear his lungs of the putrid stench, he glanced sideways to Michael.

"I know that look, Rich, but we have to call the police about this," Michael stated soberly. "This isn't exactly an everyday occurrence."

"Nothing's ever an everyday occurrence for me, you should know that," he looked carefully at the small picture of Hollie and touched the mysterious book before thinking for a second.

"I think you might want to wash your hands, whatever you do," Michael casually offered, noticing the smears of blood on Richards's hands. "You should have really left things alone. You do know that's evidence tampering, right?"

Richard looked up abruptly. "Evidence? Evidence for what? The police couldn't make head nor tails of what's going on here. What're they going to do when they find out the guy who did all this is technically dead but just happens to be wandering the streets with half a face! *I* don't even know what it all means," he closed his eyes and gritted his teeth. "What I do know is that Chris didn't do this, not willingly. At least…I don't want anyone thinking that he did!"

"There's no way around it," Michael quietly said. "If he was anything like you and it meant protecting what you do then I think he would have wanted you to call it in. The police will deal with it in their own way but the people who matter will know he's innocent. At the end of the day, that's all that matters."

Richard raised his head and looked to Michael remorsefully. "Do it," he closed the door and looked at the picture of Hollie again as Michael began to dial. "They need to do what they need to do... and so do I."

IV - Desert of Desolation

The wise man's eyes are in his head; but the fool walketh in darkness...

-Ecclesiastes 2:14

The Border World was one thing. When falling asleep most people slip in and out of it and never even realise. Those moments just before you lose consciousness, when the world slows down and nothing feels as it should. The only difference is that Medians can go there at will.

The Desert was something else, though. Few had ever willingly gone there. Even fewer had come back. It's a stopping place for spirits with unfinished business, those who want to try and get back to our world. None of them spend any more than a few minutes there, they either find a way back to the Border World or are sent to the Other Side.

The only exceptions are us. Medians never go easily to the Other Side and this would be no different if I was right about Hollie. But there was only one way I was about to find out, I would have to do something every fibre of my being told me not to. I would have to die.

The moon rose high in the night sky, casting a thin veil of light across the quiet side street. On the corner opposite to Chris' apartment two dark outlines lingered in the shade, seemingly waiting.

"What time is it?" Richard asked faintly, breaking the distant droning of the bypass. "They should have been here by now."

Michael pulled back his sleeve and quickly looked at his watch. "Twenty past ten," he dropped his arm and sighed. "Maybe we shouldn't wait around like this. You must know how suspicious this looks."

"Twenty past ten…Just under twenty six hours," Michael squinted slightly at him and opened his mouth to say something but quickly closed it again and turned away. "I just feel I should be here for this," he paused again and looked out across the street. "Things have changed, Mike… I guess you need to know a few things," he rubbed his face and tried to think of the best way to proceed. "You remember me telling you that Halloween was nothing?" he grimaced slightly. "I lied. It's a time when the lines between worlds blur and spirits can cross over than easier than usual. What I do-"

"I know," stated Michael abruptly. "I know everything you do, how deep you get yourself. I even know why you tried to hide it from me. It's because I'm like you, isn't it? I'm a Median…Or will eventually be one, at least," he looked into Richards eyes through the haze of night and felt somehow vindicated that there was no response.

"We'll see," Richard finally said as a police car pulled up on the other side of the street. "There are things *they* understand," he tilted his head in the direction of the Police exiting their squad car, "and there are things we understand. But some things that nobody can understand. Just remember that," he craned his head into the street and watched the authorities enter Chris' apartment block.

Michael sank down to the ground, his back against the wall. He was becoming convinced that Richard was toying with him, that nothing would ever please him, that everything would be forever scrutinised and that he would never be accepted as an equal.

"Come on, we're leaving," Richard said quickly, helping Michael up from the ground, pulling him closer for a second. "Just remember something else. I am proud of you. Don't you ever think I'm not," he hurried off down the street, making certain to keep to the shadows as Michael smiled gently before following.

Twenty six hours. Something told me that if Millaian was going to do something, he was going to do it on All Hallows. If he managed to get his hands on the last victim by then, there would be no stopping him. Twenty six hours was the longest amount of 'safe' time I had left. Even so, that scarcely made me feel any better, especially with what I was about to do.

I hadn't seen Lancer in years and although I knew Chris wanted me to visit him, something had been stopping me, pushing it to the back of my mind to forget. But I had no choice now.

They hadn't walked for long before Richard abruptly stopped and looked across the street at a boarded up and decrepit church. He gestured his hand towards it, forcing Michael to turn sharply and rush back towards Richard, having breezed past him in his hurry.

Apart from the boarded windows the building was half covered with scaffolding. The only parts of the sandstone walls not covered with thick moss and ivy were crumbling away, if not missing at all, replaced by shoddy bricking.

"This place?" Michael asked dismissively, grimacing at the building, "but…It's-"

"I appreciate the irony. Apparently, so does Lancer," he looked up at the precarious steeple which was missing the majority of its tiles and threatened to collapse at any time. "At least, that's what he used to say."

Michael looked sharply at Richard. "Lancer? That's who we're going to see?" Richard nodded quickly. "I didn't think he really existed"

Richard tore his gaze away from the chapel, his face awash with bewilderment. His mouth hung half open as words developed in the back of his throat. "You know about Lancer?"

"Only rumours. They're more myths really. About him being a Seer and all," Michael began to stammer under that scrutinising gaze before coughing awkwardly. "Just stories though."

Richard was quietly impressed yet ever so slightly disturbed. How had Michael found all this out on his own, even when Richard had tried so hard to prevent him from doing so? It all made him wonder just what else he knew.

"You could call him a Seer," he answered finally, "to the extent he can see beyond this world into the Median plane, yes. Apart from that he's just another guy," he paused for a few seconds before sighing and shaking his head slightly. "Though he does dabble in fields I wouldn't dream of. He's rather the eccentric, you see, so keep your wits about you," he looked back up at the old chapel. "This is it, though," added Richard flatly, "not much to look at, I realise, but that's how he likes it. Always did," he finished quietly before striding towards a doorway obscured by a loose, graffiti strewn plank of chipboard.

He prised away the board, sheering loose sand grains from the wall which drifted down through the dust filled air. Leaning against the board when he was done, Richard looked back at Michael. "So, are you coming?" he turned back to the chapel again and disappeared into the dark opening.

Michael smiled briefly and raced towards the doorway while Richard pushed open a second, much more stable, iron gate into a reasonably well lit chapel hall. The hall was gutted of everything that would have once defined it as any type of church. The pews, organ, pulpit; they had all been ripped out, leaving a much larger space than the building should have presented. The walls were lined with lamps and bright spotlights stood over piles of crates, making the chapel resemble more a warehouse than a place of worship. At the far end, atop the alter step, was a high backed wooden seat, a lone silhouette seated silently.

Michael stepped forward quickly, peering at the figure but was harshly pushed back. "Why is he just sat there?"

"He doesn't sleep, just spends the whole night wandering," replied Richard quietly.

"But he's just sat there," he stepped back realising that even here he may be in danger.

Richard slowly began to approach Lancer, his arms slightly outstretched as though he were feeling for something ahead of him.

"Just because he isn't moving doesn't mean he's not off somewhere else," he turned back to Michael for a second and smirked, knowing full well that he had thoroughly confused him. "Problem is that he doesn't much like being disturbed," he edged closer to the alter step, waving his arms all the way until his fingers suddenly sparked and ghostly waves drifted away from them. "Watch yourself," he waved his arm back towards Michael with his other still pointing towards the chair, "he's not the most agreeable person in the world." In the chair Lancers eyes flicked towards Richard and two of the ghostly forms drifted down to his sides.

"Your back," the thick, dark, German accent quickly drew Richards attention back to the alter step, his eyes wide open, "I didn't think you'd ever return."

"Well, you know," Richard began as Michael approached cautiously, "not even you could ever predict me."

Lancer looked to Richards' side and to the scared lad coming up behind him. He squinting at him before looking back. "This much I know to be true."

The ghosts drifted forwards and seemed to examine the interlopers briefly, forcing Michael to become rigidly still, before drifting away silently.

"Come, Richard…And the prodigy," he looked down to Richards side again. "After all, what else could he possibly be for you to bring him here, of all places," Lancer flicked his eyes around the building and then down at Richard and Michaels still figures. "Don't be afraid, Rich. I suspect that anything I could do to you cannot possibly be as bad as whatever it is you actually want from me."

Richard reached forward and through where the ghostly barrier had been then took a tentative step up. He breathed a quiet sigh and continued several, more confident, steps towards Lancer. "Maybe I had you wrong. Maybe you can predict me."

"What is it you want, Richard?" he opened out his hands welcomingly. "Such a long time, it must be something important for you to finally come back."

"I need to go there, Lancer. I need to go to The Desert," Richard stated quickly, despite how much he wanted not to.

Lancer grinned and pushed himself from the chair, starting to walk slowly forwards. "I never thought I would hear those words from you, not again. You do realise what it entails, do you not?" he carried on knowing full well what the answer would be.

"Yes, I remember. This is something that needs to be done, though," he stared straight at Lancer who gazed back casually but then suddenly flicked his eyes towards Michael.

"The boy doesn't know," Lancer began to walk to Richards' side and tried to reach out but his arm was grabbed and pulled away sharply.

"He knows enough," Richard threw the seized arm aside and took a step in front of Michael.

"Perhaps but I feel he fails to understand the gravity of what he would involve himself in," Lancer rubbed his aged hands together and turned back to Richard. "Do you, for that matter?"

"I know exactly what I need to."

"I know the only thing you could possibly find there is absence. An emptiness and loneliness beyond compare...Unless..." he turned around and started to walk back towards his chair, "...It is not? Are you hoping to find something there, my friend? Someone?" he chuckled faintly as Richard stepped forward and opened his mouth but was silenced by Lancers arm being thrown up. "I know of this individual...In such desolation I feel any slightest disturbance," he breathed in heavily and seemed to savour the thought of the 'disturbance.' "And this was..." he closed his eyes and breathed deeply again, "so powerful."

Michael slowly placed a hand on Richards' shoulder prompting him to turn quickly. "What does he mean he can feel it?"

Richard spoke as quietly as he dared, not knowing exactly why but clearing possessing a deep fear of Lancer. "Seers. They're the guardians of the Median World. They can see all who pass through it. I thought you said you knew this!"

"I said just stories!"

"Indeed we *can* see all!" stated Lancer loudly, swinging around. "A whole world at our fingertips. Such a wonderful thing you may think. It is truly not," he rushed back down towards the pair again, right up to stare Michael in the eye. "A world so full of emptiness, scratching at your senses every hour of every day-" he quickly turned to Richard, grasping his arms tightly. "You Medians have it easy! For me every second is a lifetime's insanity, the endless void pouring through my mind, dominating my sleepless nights!" he seemed to regain control of himself and let go of Richards arms, removing them as though he didn't know how they had gotten there. "Then again, you are aware of this...You've been there."

"And I need to go again," Richard replied tentatively, "you said yourself she's there. I need to bring her back."

Lancer shook his head and rubbed his face. "*She* is something else. You know I can't even be sure about bringing you back, let alone two of you," he looked to the ground and shook his head again. "And even if I could, I'm not sure if I should. It is different, Richard...*She* is different."

Richard suddenly saw something glint in Lancers eyes and stepped towards him, looking closer. "You've felt it haven't you? The presence in the Border World."

"That is your jurisdiction, my friend," he replied firmly, gritting his yellowed teeth, "it has nothing to do with me."

"But you know. You've felt him. He crossed the desert, didn't he?" He thought for a second, "and you knew I'd come...For her..." he pointed an accusing finger sharply at Lancer. "Come on! You're not stupid, far from it! You know she's in danger and it doesn't matter whether she's here or the Other Side, the worse possible place she could be is the desert!"

Lancer hung his head, wiping his face. "This presence you speak of. It is nothing like I've ever felt. Such pure power and raw hatred; there's not a Seer that couldn't have felt it," he raised his head and flicked his eyes between the two. "I heard him, Richard. I heard his thoughts as though they were my own...Such darkness..." A tear began to drip from his face as he spoke. "The void filled with hatred and a haze of malice. He spoke of Christopher and the poles of balance. Cause and effect, ying and yang, good and evil. He spoke of his opposite. Of you."

Richard looked deep into Lancers eyes and saw something in them he had never seen from a Seer. He saw an unmitigated, unrelenting fear which ran so deep that he could never possibly begin to understand it. If Millaian could do this to a Seer then he dared not think about what else he could do. "It's alright," he ventured.

"It's alright to be scared, even for you." He quickly looked back to Michael, now so petrified that his eyes had become bloodshot.

"I'm ok," Michael whispered, nodded reassuringly before looking back to Lancer.

"You have to help me bring her back, "Richard continued. "He's out there, Lancer. He's out there right now with Chris' body and she might be our only chance to stop him before he ends up doing god only knows what."

There was silence for some time as the old man considered Richards words. Eventually Lancer stood up straight again, wiping the tears from his face and breathing in deeply. "Of course," he stated flatly, casually raising an eyebrow and chuckling shortly to himself. "I would be only too glad to oblige," he finished as he began to walk off towards a shadowed door at the side of the chapel hall.

Richard put his hand on Michaels shoulder lightly and patted gently. "I have every faith in you. I know you'll be able to do whatever you have to," he patted his shoulder again and started following Lancer but was quickly stopped again.

"Wait, do what? What do you expect me to do?"

"You'll know, don't worry. For now, I think it would be better for you to stay out here. Don't be afraid, Lancer's got this place pretty well protected. I think they should know you're trust worthy enough by now," he smiled and looked to the rafters before continuing on to the side door.

Michael slowly gazed upwards to the roof and couldn't believe his eyes. The entire roof space was aglow with a brilliant white from ghostly spectres drifting around the supporting beams. He remembered reading about these things; the protectors of the precious living. "Guardians?" laughed Michael in awe of the wonderful sight, "I'd say they were more like angels."

Lancer forced aside a rusted bolt on the old wooden door and pushed it open, making its thick iron supports clang on the stone wall.

"I can't say I've missed this thing," said Richard sombrely, stepping into the room ahead of Lancer.

Before him was a half blackened steel table with leather straps and harnesses, positioned for the restraint of a person's limbs. Beside the table was a strange looking device sat atop on old medical cabinet with several thick cables and coloured wires looping around it. Within it was housed a number of old car batteries, dirtied from years of use and dried battery acid encrusting their seals.

"Could have at least cleaned it up a bit," Richard casually offered, continuing to examine the room.

Around the dingy cell were low shelves full of strange vials and implements he cared not to know the purpose of.

"I think you should just lie down," Lancer answered flatly, taking a jaw ended wire from the knotted jumble and clamping it firmly to a pylon on the underside of the table. "You'll want to relax during the process. Sudden separation can be a little-" he clamped another wire onto a second pylon and moved to Richards's side.

"I get the idea," Richard finished, doing as he was instructed. "It's not like you forget these things," he took a deep breath and clenched his fists nervously as Lancer reached for the restraints. "Are those really necessary, though?"

"I'm afraid so," he strapped an arm tightly into the leather bond and moved on to his feet, securing them as harshly as he had the arm. "Trust me, it's for your own safety."

"Safe? I don't think there could be a less operative word for what you're about to do then 'safe,'"

Lancer briefly acknowledged this as he fastened the last restraint in place and moved back to the machine.

"Sure they're tight enough?" Richard added, tugging at the straps. "Don't want me getting loose, do we?"

"Just relax," Lancer stated again, flipping several switches on the contraption, causing it to emit a low pitched buzz, "this might hurt a little."

"Says the master of the understatement," Richard breathed in deeply and clenched his teeth as Lancer took hold of two rubber handled paddles from the device. He quickly touched them together, creating a bright spark, before placing them just short of Richards temples.

"Any last words?" Lancer asked, chuckling lightly and quickly pressing the cold metal against Richards's skin before he could respond.

Immediately he started to convulse against the restraints, writhing against the electricity now surging through his body. He continued to thrash against the leather bounds for some time, eventually throwing his head back against the metal slab with a sickly crack. After a split second of blissful calm Richards body was suddenly lifted, contorted, into the air by a final pulse of static and he let loose a harrowing scream to rival that of a rabid wolverine.

Outside, the haunting wail pierced Michael to his very core. Without a second thought it made him race towards its origin, barely allowing his mind a chance to process the terrible sensation.

He threw open the door just as the screaming ceased only to see Richard's body fall limp and Lancer slowly withdraw the paddles.

"What the hell have you done?!" Michael yelled, grabbing Lancer by the shoulder and throwing him harshly against the cabinet with a clatter. "You've killed him!"

"I would prefer not to hurt you, boy," he replied calmly, trying to hold the still buzzing conductors away from them both, "so if you would allow me to-"

Michael snatched at one of Lancers hands and pushed the paddle close to his face while holding the other away. "Why did you do it?" he growled, resisting his urge to complete the circuit using Lancers face. "Tell me!" he shouted finally.

"The current will do nothing to me," he casually pushed away Michaels grip with the least amount of effort and forced him to the ground. "Trust me, I've tried," he quickly turned and flicked the machines switches back to their 'Off' positions and sighed gently, placing the paddles down. "This is distressing, I realise, and for this I forgive you your abrupt actions but you have to understand that you have been entrusted with a great responsibility. You must ensure the protection of the body."

"You what?" Michael stated in disgust. "After what you just did, you talk about 'protection?'"

"Not *his* body. There is another whom you must retrieve."

"This is some kind of nightmare, it has to be," Michael said quickly, grabbing his head wildly

"It is not," replied Lancer flatly. "Be aware this was of Richards choosing. In order to pass into the desert the body must not anchor the spirit to this world."

Michael stumbled to his feet again, thinking for a second and suddenly came to a realisation. "You mean the Median World? I didn't think it was possible to *really* go there. I thought it was a metaphor... Or something." Michaels brow narrowed as he tried to understand everything that was going on.

"Oh, it is quite possible. It is in returning that difficulties arise," he walked to the large steel slab and began to undo the restraints that held Richard.

"'And for the ones who live astride the worlds; the sore silence prevails before peace,'" quoted Michael. "I read that once. It means Medians can stay there longer than most, doesn't it?"

"Smart boy. I see why he let you come here," Lancer smiled shallowly and unhooked the last leather bond. "It is a great power when seeking that which is hidden...Or lost"

"So that's who he's looking for? He thinks she's like us?...A Median."

"Like you, my boy, like you," Lancer placed a hand firmly on Michaels shoulder. "I wouldn't have let him do this if she wasn't there. You see, Richard isn't the only one who can step between the worlds. Lets just say that if some adversity were to get to her first then..." he shook his head, trying to repress the feeling. "Such evil was never meant to exist."

"That zombie...that thing Chris turned into?"

"Millaian...He has found his host but will not remain there, he cannot. Soon, if we can not stop him, his plan will come to pass. I do not wish to experience what will happen if it does."

Michael paused fearfully for a second. "So where is Richard now?" he asked tentatively, changing the topic.

"Right next to you," Lancer looked just to the side of Michael and grinned making him glance around wildly. "You won't be able to see him. Only I have that pleasure. It's the-" he thought for a second if to use the word 'Gift' or 'Curse' but came to the conclusion that neither was suitable, "-Bequest of the Seers, to see the unseen, for those lost in torment. To forever witness The Desert."

Michael sighed heavily, growing tired of Lancers exposition. "Yeah, that's all very well and good but was electrocution *really* the best way? Wouldn't, say, Nitrous Oxide have been much more appropriate? You know, a painless method?"

"The spirit must be driven from the body quickly if we are to stop this evil in time. A shock of great intensity is the only way to do so without physically harming his body." He looked to Michael's side again and seemed to listen for a moment or two. "We must hurry. Richard has tasked you with a vital objective," he began to rush around the room, inspecting seemingly random bottles until he came to a small vial containing an off yellow serum. Quickly he turned back to Michael, grabbing a sealed syringe as he went and rushed forward, forcing the items into Michael's hands.

"Wait!" he barked, stopping Lancer in his tracks. "What does all this mean?"

Lancer looked to Michael's side again and sighed solemnly, nodding slightly. "You have to bring her back. This serum-" he pointed firmly to the vial now poised clumsily in Michaels hands, "-will reanimate her body, reverse any rigor mortis and prepare her for the merging. Richard will find her spirit. If he is right, and to go to the desert he must be pretty damn sure, he'll be able to sense her and bring her here...I'm afraid so must you. I can then re-merge her body and spirit and, for lack of a better way to describe it..." he thought for a second whether he really wanted to say it in such a clumsy fashion but finally relented. "Bring her back to life."

Michael stared, wide eyed at him, not fully sure he wanted to participate any longer. "So just find the body, inject her with this stuff and bring her back?" he reiterated simply.

"Basically, yes," replied Lancer, now thinking the simple approach would have probably been better in the first place. He started to usher Michael out of the small room, all the time fumbling with the items he had been given. "Do you think he can handle this task?" he asked, turning back to where Michael had been stood.

Across the border world and through the astral boundaries Richard stood. To Lancer, he was as a shadowy aura against a dark and desolate reality inhabited now by fear and a deep, empty loneliness.

"He can do it," came Richards faded echo of a voice, "it might just take him a while to get used to it." He looked around the place, a washed out world with the air tinted a depressed shade of brown from an eternity of neglect and no real purpose in the cosmos. "I could never get used to this place, you know," he sighed quietly. "But I guess no-one could, that's the point."

"You won't be there for long," replied Lancer firmly, "either way about it."

Richard adjusted his jacket casually and tried to take a deep breath but getting nothing but void. "I had better be off then," he finished, giving Lancer a meaningful nod before exiting hurriedly.

Lancer lowered his head slightly, possibly the only one who was fully aware of how pressing the situation really was and let two near silent words drift from his lips. "Good Luck."

In the desert, nothing felt real and nothing existed as it should have in the real world. The gutted chapel had a harrowing absence of any sound. A deathly silence that chilled to the bone. The guardians no longer drifted about the rafters, their absence depriving the space of that warm sense of safety that could only be truly appreciated now it was gone.

Richard strode with conviction towards the door, trying to block out the overwhelming desolation calling out from every inch of this place. It was no help, though, for even his thoughts were empty. The encroaching voices of a thousand lost souls that constantly tormented him had fallen silent, unable or unwilling to peruse him back across the void, closer to whence they had come.

He carefully pressed his fingers against the iron portal to the outside. It was ice cold to the touch and made him shiver, forcing him to withdraw his hand. Finally he heaved open the doorway and stepped out into a gloomy daylight. Richard hated how, in this place, it was never truly night. He looked to the sky but there was no sun, and no night to come. There was only a thick sprawl of dusky clouds emitting their dull, sickly glare.

Trying to put this all out of his mind, Richard closed his eyes and, in the emptiness, searched for her. As he did he couldn't help but think that on some level this place was where he, and all Medians alike, were strongest. They were free from the endless threat of spirits from the Other Side, free to think clearly, and sense things through the eternity of silence that they never could in the din of the real world.

He slowly opened his eyes and realised what he had been thinking, cursing himself for it. Neither he nor any Median ever wanted to be in that place but it was an undeniable fact that it had a power over them, one so strong it could change even their deepest thoughts. It was their celestial home, the true place of the Medians, the root of what they were and all that they knew. It allowed for Richard not only to know that Hollie was there but exactly where and what she was.

He looked up and down the dull, deserted street hoping that she was, indeed, as important as they thought her to be. Eventually he set off down the street as fast as he could walk, knowing what this place could do to him and how much danger they could both be in.

V - The Wretched

For I know that thou wilt bring me to death, and to the house appointed for all living

-Job 30:20

For every being of true goodness and light in the universe, there must be something of equal evil and darkness. This was most apparent in everyday life. For every old woman helped across the road there would be one whose bag was stolen. It was also true of the shadowy worlds which separate reality, with whispered beings lurking in the dark regions of the emptiest desert of them all. Few had observed these things first hand and fewer had returned to tell of them. They were corrupted spirits of the long past trapped between the walls of this world and the next, driven insane by their torturous plights. Many despised them, feared them, but I pitied them; the Wretched condemned and damned.

A dark cloud dragged slowly across the bright, not quite full moon and trailed off into the night sky. It obscured even the stars able to pierce the city's yellow haze, making the night seem that much darker. Michael looked down from the sky and sat back heavily in the car seat, thinking about what he was about to do. Looking across at the hospital again, he could only consider what would happen if he was caught.

Bodysnatching was a high crime, not to mention an utterly despicable action unto its self. He tried to remind himself that it was for a greater good and that lives could be saved by going through with it. It hardly did anything to ease his mind, however, by now he'd seen enough dead bodies get up and start walking around for one lifetime and wasn't keen to see another. Come to that, Millaian was still out there. Michael just prayed that he was far away by now. Better still would be if he was back in the land of the dead but then, he supposed, zombies weren't known for being the easiest beings to put back down.

Eventually swallowing his fear, he opened the car door and stepped cautiously into a yellow pool of light cast by the street lamps overhead and looked over at the hospital, sighing. It was no longer just himself he needed to fear for but all those who would suffer if Millaian were able to succeed in his plan.

He closed the door and, with the anxiety rising in his chest, he began to walk towards the building.

Thoughts raced through his mind of how he was going to go about getting into the place. He doubted very much that Richard's fire alarm trick would work a second time and he simply did not have the mindset needed to break into anywhere, let alone a hospital.

As he neared the A&E entrance it started to become apparent that a distraction may not even be required. Panicked people were rushing around, some with large, clotted gashes across their arms and clothes smeared with blood. Getting closer he could see a body sprawled limply over a gurney. His throat was slit and he seemed to have several deep stab marks through his chest. Michael turned away, covering his mouth, and nearly walked into one of the nurses rushing by.

"You alright?" she said hurriedly. "He didn't get you, did he?"

Michael looked at her sideways, slowly removing his hand from his mouth, shaking uncontrollably. "What? ...Uh, no," he thought for a second and looked at her properly, remembering that there were more important questions to be asked. "Who? What happened here?"

"A guy went psycho with a scalpel in there, don't know how many people he killed in the end but he managed to mess up the chem lab before he escaped. Whole ward's a biohazard now!" She looked about suspiciously and came to an otherwise obvious conclusion. "Wait, you're not a patient!"

"I have family in there," spurted Michael quickly. "I came as soon as I heard something had happened," he paused for a second to assess if the nurse had believed him. To his surprise she apparently had. "Where did he go?" he ventured. "This psycho guy?"

"I don't know. The police reckon they have a trace on him. Not that you could miss him, he's supposedly got half his face missing, although I didn't see him myself," she looked around again but this time quickly rushed off to help with a patient.

Michael was left with a chill creeping up his spine. Part of him had hoped this was all a bad dream or a figment of his imagination but now that hope was gone. This was Millaians wrath and it was going to continue until he was stopped once and for all.

He worked his way as silently as he could between the crowd of distressed patients and doctors alike and slipped into the deserted reception area. The swing doors to the ward were now crisscrossed with yellow tape emblazoned with biohazard symbols. Beyond, hazard suit clad figures shimmered behind the tinted glass. He looked carefully behind the reception desk. There was an un-taped and most likely overlooked plywood door back there. Michael knew very well that the door was probably locked tight and left him no recourse but to break in. On reflection, he concluded that, given the gravity of the situation, a level of civil disobedience may have been acceptable. Besides, it was nothing compared to the intended act of body snatching.

Michael swiftly clambered over the reception desk and tried the door which was, as he had expected, locked firmly. Without a second thought, he looked around for something to force the door with. He scrambled through draws and filing cabinets but found nothing but clipboards and flimsy folders. Eventually he stopped and looked carefully at the door, then down at his feet. Bracing himself against the side wall, he threw a foot as hard as he could towards the latch. Immediately the lock splintered and flew off, leaving the door to swing open wildly into the opposite plaster wall, digging a considerable hole in the weak partition. Realising that this hadn't been the quietest and that someone would no doubt investigate any second, Michael started off along the staff corridor as fast as he dared.

Michael had never wanted to return to that or any other morgue, having neglected to note how to get there. As it was then, his less than subtle mode of entry had ultimately been fortuitous. Signs lined the staff corridors directing to places the public were never meant to visit, including the morgue.

Hurrying along the corridors, following the signs the best he could, Michael could hear the muffled voices of suited inspectors growing ever closer.

Instead of trying to flee their approach, he decided to duck behind a nearby partition and tried to control his anxious breathing. As much as he had tried to put it out of his mind, the fear of those spilt toxins had consumed his thoughts. He had to know just how dangerous they were and whether he, himself, would be long for this world if he stumbled upon them. Without a more reasonable option, his only choice was to find out from the only source available, a source that could also bring his task to a premature end.

Footsteps grew closer until voices were discernible. "...over the place. We were lucky this time; sectors 3 through 7 are clean. Looks like the toxic stuff was contained to the lab." There was a short burst of static and a blip the words were directed into a radio, most likely to the Police or Hazard Control Agency operatives stationed outside.

"Roger. Continue with recon and keep us appraised. Cleanup crew are inbound," the mostly garbled response came across the radio before another blast of static and a bleep.

"Oh well, looks like we're all done here," said a different voice.

"I should bloody well hope so too, supposed to be at home with the wife and kids to..." the voice faded away as they continued on down the corridor, out of earshot again.

Michael slumped against the wall and breathed a sigh of relief before carrying on towards the morgue. As he went, it became apparent that the lights were becoming dimmer and eventually ceased to work altogether, the corridor lit only by the glow from offices and adjacent rooms.

Although his better sense was screaming for him to turn back, he pushed forward until he finally rounded a corner to his destination. Almost immediately he was halted by the visage of a person stood halfway down the next hall. Retreating back around the corner, Michael stood for a few moments, pressed flat against the wall, hoping that he hadn't been seen. He stood in silence for several more seconds, his heart pounding so hard against his chest that he felt it may give him away. The seconds continued to tick by, slow enough to be eternities unto themselves until a word drifted gently around the corner to Michaels ringing ears.

"Hello?" The voice seemed scared, lost almost, but with a relief that came only with the breaking of solitude. "I know you're there...Please come out," the voice began to tremor with fear. "There's something dark here...And it's coming back to get me...To get all of us."

"I'm here," stated Michael softly, without thinking. He didn't know why but he stepped from the shadows and began walking towards the figure. All the time it remained motionless, silhouetted against the still functioning lights at the end of the hall.

"Help me! Please god, help me!" the man pleaded in terror as Michael continued to approach. "He will complete himself and then return for us all!"

"Who?" The question was asked even though the answer was known but still there came no response.

As what little light there was drew across the man's face it became apparent that he was a young doctor although his features had become long and drained of all colour. His white coat was now dulled a dirty brown and had streaks of blood across it, the result of three deep stab wounds through his chest. This had been Millaians work. Soon a sickening realisation dawned upon Michael. This had been the first doctor who had found him. The first of what would soon to be many victims.

He composed himself and turned slowly to the door of the morgue, taking hold of the handle firmly and, breathing a deep, fear-fraught breath, opened it. Just inside lay the body of the young doctor, his coat dyed red with his own blood and his face twisted into a vision of horror.

"Is that me?" asked the doctor quietly, unsure what was transpiring.

Michael faced him head on and knew what he had to do. There was no doubt anymore, he had taken the final steps towards being a true Median and knew instinctively what to do.

"It's time to let go," he finally replied calmly, no longer afraid of the shadowy dreams or apparitions in the night, for he now knew that there were much worse things to be afraid of. "Once you do, you'll be safe," he went to place a reassuring hand on the mans shoulder but thought better of it once remembering that he wasn't entirely there. "Trust me, there's nothing to worry about on the Other Side."

After a moments contemplation, the doctor nodded shallowly and closed his eyes, his shape rippling and beginning to drift away. His being was scattered, taken like dust in the wind, leaving a faint echoed voice on the air which came back to Michael and whispered simply, "thank you."

Smiling slightly, Michael at last entered the morgue, carefully stepping over the body, and headed for a specific door in the freezer cabinet. He stopped for a second before pulling open the small door, unsure of how he knew which one Hollie was in with such certainty.

Stepping back, he looked carefully at the whole wall of metal doors but still came to that same one. He could sense it was her. Some residual trace of her past life had left a dull imprint on his newly horizoned mind. He quickly pulled at the handle, forcing the door open and allowing the cold, metal body-plate inside to slip quickly out.

On it laid a black body bag, apparently unaffected by the freezing temperatures but still cold to the touch. He grabbed the zip and, after a moment more of hesitation, pulled it some way down, revealing the body concealed inside. It was indeed a woman, her skin frosty and turned a faint shade of blue by the sub-zero temperatures.

Michael scrambled in his coat to find the picture Richard had taken from Chris' apartment and held it up to her face. Apart from the distinct colour change of the corpse and lack of any identifiable expression, it was her. He, once again, began to search his coat for the syringe and vial of serum with which he would attempt to revive her. Once found, he clumsily managed to draw the liquid into the syringe and, after pausing again to assess the best way he should go about doing it, pinched the sterile needle into her frozen arm, injecting its contents.

Richard came to a halt at the crossroads of what, in the real world, would have been a busy street, even as late in the day as it was. He grinned briefly at the idea that he was stood in the middle of a busy intersection and wasn't causing all out chaos. Better yet, he wasn't even at any risk of being run over and killed. It wasn't simply that there weren't any cars to endanger him here but, in all the ways that mattered, he was already dead, immune from that which had already occurred. His grin fell away as he realised that there was a good chance he was going to stay that way if he didn't speed up his efforts and his thoughts turned quickly back to the matter at hand. He looked about the empty street with the cold air of absence weighing increasingly upon him.

Buildings stood here only as a testament to mans echoed legacy. It was something that, like all things, would eventually wither and crumble. The only reminder that it lived still was the occasional shimmer of a car, static in place for several days, having imprinted itself upon the fabric of this reality.

Richard had never fully understood how this could happen. How long did standing fixtures of the living world need in order to press through to this plane? How was it even achieved in the first place? None the less, despite its apparent impossibility, it was. Buildings, roads, even furniture providing it had been there long enough, they all eventually left their mark, the ghosts of life.

He continued to gaze about the street. She was here somewhere but now too close to pinpoint exactly where. Ahead of him, a figure appeared in the middle of the street but before it could know where it was, it faded away again. It was just another soul passing through on its way to the Other Side, not able to know or even acknowledge where it was before being sped on again across the existential plains.

Richard continued to stare at the buildings, not knowing where to start but acutely aware that he didn't have time to systematically search them all. Closing his eyes, his thoughts drifted out into the void of emotion. He knew there was a good chance that it wouldn't work but a long time ago he had been taught that in the absence of all else, the smallest echo could be deafening to a well-trained ear. Having no idea what this had meant until his first trip to the Median World, he quickly came to realise that all Medians are natural Empaths. Empathy was the root of their ability to commune with the Other Side, the understanding those who had come from there and it was just another one of the traits this place happened to enhance.

Richards mind drifted around the street, probing into every storey of the buildings around him, finding only an increasing sense of harrowing emptiness. The tormenting feeling grew within him, attacking his primal fears and was about to force him to stop when suddenly something hit him. An overwhelming sense of sorrow traced through his body and convulsed him into weeping.

Upon composing himself, he turned sharply to the street he had just walked down and ran towards the second building along from the intersection. He forced his way through the main door, shattering its imprinted image on this world, and rushed up a set of stairs, knowing exactly which apartment to head to. Only stopping once he reached an apartment on the third floor, Richard paused, panting heavily, and inspected the door carefully.

The feeling was stronger than ever here but, despite being one of the deepest miseries he had ever felt, it was somehow comforting for it meant that he was not alone in this place.

He moved to take the door handle and thought back to something Chris had once told him. 'The worst of feeling is better than no feeling at all'. He nodded to himself and slowly opened the door, stepping into the apartment.

From the far end of the entrance hall came the sound of sobbing which Richard quickly followed into the living room, finding Hollie huddled in the far corner. She was mumbling incoherently amongst her sniffled sobs and holding her knees so tight that her hands had turned white. She did, indeed, resemble her picture, only now looking as if she had been through hell and back. For a moment Richard reflected that, to some extent, she had.

He stepped closer to her and reached out a hand carefully. "It's alright, Hollie, you're not alone anymore."

"No!" she snapped abruptly. "You're not real! Just another one of them!" she began to rock back and forth repeating the words 'not real' over and over.

He thought about who 'they' may be but decided that getting her away was his main priority. "I assure you I am as real as I possibly can be," he stopped for a second and considered what he had just said, "in this place at least," he added quietly. "I'm here to help you, take you back."

"They say they want to help me too...They lie!" she raised her head towards Richard and tilted it slightly, wiping a tear from her face. "But...you don't look like them...You look normal."

Richard stepped closer to her and gently placed a hand on her shoulder. "You're in danger here, I'm going to take you home." What she had spoken of had certainly peaked his curiosity but, for the moment, he managed to sway his attention back to the more pressing issues.

"No!" She squirmed back from him, against the wall. "That's where they were. I thought I could escape them but they followed me, I don't know how." She calmed and looked at Richard carefully. "You're not one of them, though, are you?"

"Who are 'They?'" he finally asked. "*What* are they?"

She turned her head and gazed into the open room. "They are the starless night...The plague of the void..." she spoke slowly, transfixed upon something in the room and raised a shaking arm, finger outstretched. "They are his dark minions."

Richard spun round and backed into the corner as he laid eyes on something he never truly believed existed. A myth of the underworld and what he had hoped never to face. "Reavers!"

Reavers were a mythical demon of the border worlds, twisted amalgamations of outcast spirits, formed into horrific visions of the void between life and death. Stories told of them prowling silently through the borders, seeking lost souls to corrupt and make theirs.

Three stood hooded and silent, near motionless other than slightly swaying in a haunting, simultaneous fashion. Each looked different, their spirits merged in different ways but all were a sickening, charred red, as though their flesh had been stripped and burnt.

One stood with a single twin jointed leg aside a normal one. Sharpened elongate bones protruded from its elbows and a third limb reached out from inside its half exposed rib cage.

The other two had otherwise normal limbs, only with their finger tips sharpened to needle points. One even seemed to have faces pressing up against the inside of its chest. None of the creatures faces were distinguishable, only dull yellow glows emitting from beneath their hoods.

Hollie gradually opened her hand out and waved across each one in turn, leaning forward slightly as Richard tried to pull her away. "Seeker..." she stated across the most human of them. "Carrier..." she waved across the second most human and gazed at the faces in its chest sorely before moving on to the last one. She grimaced at this abomination of a creature and darkened her voice, "...Hunter."

Richard stared at her for a second, hardly able to believe she knew so much about their hierarchy but eventually pulled her back and managed to manoeuvre himself in front of her. He was unsure if this would make any kind of difference if they attacked but at least it was something.

"From what I know of these things they can only take willing souls," warned Richard harshly. "Don't give into them!"

A hissed breath drew from the Seeker and it took a step forward, its near skeletal feet clicking hideously on the wood panelled floor. "You will...come...with us," it's chilling hissed voice was abrupt and disjointed, intended to invoke fear into everything it met. "You have...no choice."

"I think we do," Richard replied aggressively, "if you want us you'll have to take us by force...But you can't do that, can you?"

The Seeker glanced back and forth between them. "*We* do not...desire you..." it turned to Hollie sharply, "*he* does," its reply came in low, malignant tones. "You will...be taken..."

The Hunter stepped in line with The Seeker and turned slowly back towards Richard, stretching its long, sharp fingers. "You will...perish."

Hollie stood up quickly and moved in front of Richard. "Maybe it is time," she took a step forward. "I will go with you, but he must go free," she pointed backwards toward Richard.

"No!" he stood up shouting and tried to pull Hollie back again but was shrugged off.

"You have no need for him. He's just a guy," without turning she pressed Richard back, keeping him silent. "Do we have an agreement?"

"You can't do this," Richard growled finally. "I'm here to *help* you! You don't realise what's at stake. You can't go with them!"

"I know who you are," she whispered to him, "they will kill you and take me anyway..." She turned around and looked at Richard meaningfully. With the presence of another like her, Hollies solitude induced madness was beginning to and her true sight re-established itself. "I don't know what's happening to me but I know that this is not where you save me... You will, just not here."

Richard didn't know what to think but slowly took a step back regardless, concluding there wasn't any other choice.

"So, do we?" Hollie asked the Reavers as sternly as she could muster, completely terrified of what she was doing.

The Reavers were completely silent for a few more seconds until The Seeker reached up with jerked, deliberate movements, about to pull the hood from its head but stopped short and lowered the clawed hand. "Your...proposal has been...accepted."

The Carrier looked at Hollie expectantly, forcing her to begrudgingly step towards it. As she did The Hunter quickly struck out towards Richard, gripping him tightly around the neck and carrying him to the nearest window.

"No!" Hollie screamed, squirming against The Carrier as it grabbed hold of her. "You said he'd be spared!"

"He will not...be harmed..." The Seeker stated in the least reassuring way.

The Hunter raised Richard up, tightening its grip as its eyes glowed a brighter yellow. "...much," it added slyly to its counterparts statement before throwing Richard as hard as it could. It shattering the windows image on the world and left Richard to fall helplessly to the concrete street two floors below.

The Seeker looked to Hollie, its pinpoint eyes standing out against the harrowing darkness in its cowl. Eventually low hissed words slithered from the tattered hood and struck a cold, primal fear into her heart. It simply said, "you are his."

VI - The Other Side

For many are called, but few are chosen

-Matthew 22:14

Hurriedly pushing the gurney hurriedly down the corridor, it dawned on Michael that, all he had done so far had been the easy part. The challenge of getting Hollies body out of the hospital unnoticed still stood before him. He abruptly stopped and looked at the black body bag, trying not to think too much about what was inside. It was still cool to the touch and the sight of it made him agonise over if he had carried out the procedure correctly. How hard could a simple injection be, anyway? He breathed heavily, knowing he had never actually given one before and considered again if he would really able to get her out.

As if without thinking, he flicked up his arm and pushed back his sleeve in one smooth motion to look at his watch. It was closing in on two in the morning and he tried to reassure himself that at this hour it should be easy enough to go unnoticed once he was out of the hospital. Then again, he wasn't out yet and the small hours hardly meant anything to a perpetually bustling hospital. He nodded to himself slightly and started pushing the gurney again.

Knowing that he would never get out the way he had entered, he was already following signs directing to the service exit. He presumed it was where undertakers picked up their bodies so there should have been room for the gurney. At least this was the hope for, in truth, he genuinely had no idea. Either way, he wasn't leaving without that trolley for, in his mind, wheeling a body from a hospital was one thing. Carrying one out was something entirely, and much more disturbingly, different.

The gurneys wheels squeaked faintly down the polished corridor as distant sounds could be heard of staff re-entering the building, forcing Michael to pick up his pace. Eventually, having managed to keep ahead of the sprawl of staff and patients approaching, he came out onto a much wider corridor lined with several more gurneys. Some stood empty but most held body bags, occupied by those awaiting their final journey. He shuddered and cautiously continued on towards a pair of wide double doors leading to the dark car park beyond.

As he approached them he was overcome with a sense that being caught for body snatching may yet be the least of his worries for he felt as though something foul stalked him. Suddenly, the feeling became all too real and he stopped again, staring at the floor ahead.

Droplets of fresh blood trailed down the corridor, becoming more apparent as his eyes followed them towards the night. The pools soon turned to smears across the smooth surface as if a dead animal had been dragged away. The trail continued for some time and eventually lead to a single leg protruding from behind one of the stationary beds.

Despite fearing the worst, all Michael could do was press on, pretending as if he had seen nothing, but as he took a tentative step forward the fluorescent lights overhead began to flicker and failed altogether with a sharp buzz.

The sudden loss of light left him in a complete, unceasing blackness, his eyes taking far longer than he was comfortable with to acclimatise to the light spilling in through the far doors. As they did a silhouette became outlined against the sickly yellow light, its slumped and stiff appearance giving little hope of this being anyone of kind intensions.

Michael watched the lone figure for longer than he felt reasonable until it abruptly spoke in a piercing, gravelly tone. "How does it feel, my boy?"

"I know that voice," Michael mouthed, shaking steadily with fear. "It's you."

Millaian walked forward slowly, withdrawing a scalpel from the pocket of his bloodied trousers. "Yes, of course you do...But in more ways than you care to accept."

"I'll never let you have her!" he shouted, stepping in front of the gurney. "Not as long as I'm still breathing!"

Millaian laughed quietly and stopped his slow advance. "Although I would relish the opportunity to take you up on your offer, I do not need her shell. It is of no importance to me." In the darkness, a grin cut across what was left of his lips and he started to stagger towards Michael again. "I have her essence and that is all I require...No, it is not her I desire...It is you."

Michael was startled back into the gurney, making it clatter loudly. "Why?" he managed, shaking uncontrollably.

"Of course you do not know, he would have it kept from you...To keep you weak...And now his weakness has lead to his death," he pointed the scalpel accusingly at Michael, grimacing and gritting his decaying teeth. "This host felt much for you. You see, there was a bond between you, my boy...Or should I say," he took a long, wheezed breath in, truly enjoying toying with him, "my son," he finished slowly, pleased with the effect his words would bring.

Michael ran the statement through his head, trying to wrap his mind around its meaning whilst Millaians haunting grin beamed darkly through the night.

"Wait..." Michael whispered, realising that some part of him had known all along. "It's true, isn't it?" he breathed quietly, moving towards the faceless being. "He *is* my father. Richard knew it...and so did I..."

"No..." growled Millaian, backing off slightly. "You could not know, you are weak. Give up your delusions and submit or you will die."

Michael stepped up to Millaian and smiled. "No, I won't," he cocked his head and grimaced. "That's what you've wanted, isn't it? A lackey...A minion..." he looked straight back at him as it became clear. "An apprentice...You wanted someone to corrupt. Someone to make just like you..." He grew bold in his new found confidence and simply asked, "why?"

"I need not explain myself to the likes of you!" he struck out a blood smeared arm and grabbed Michael around the throat, raising him from the ground. "You will taste death for your insolence..." he tightened his grip before throwing him into the wall so hard that the plaster cracked. "For this I pity you for there is no peace on the Other Side." He once again took Michael by the throat, pressing him against the ground and raised the scalpel high, the bloodied blade glinting in what light there was. He hesitated for a second and leaned in close to Michael. The congealed rot oozed from his face, tendons in his exposed jaw tensing as he gritted his teeth.

"Why wait," Michael croaked finally, unafraid of the monster looming over him, instead seeing something in Millaian, a strength that he did not control. Michael pressed against the grip, leaning towards the blade. "Do it!" he added, knowing that he would not.

The dull light of the other world failed to even make Richard squint as he opened his eyes onto the glowing sky of the desert. The window high above shimmered indecisively, unsure whether it was still in phase with the living world or not. He sat bolt upright in the empty street as he recalled the Reavers and what they had wanted. There was little chance that she was still there, he couldn't even feel her anymore. Even so, he jumped to his feet and rushed back into the building, pounding up the flights of stairs and burst into the apartment to find that it was completely deserted. He hung his head mournfully and wiped his face, not knowing how next to proceed.

Suddenly, he looked up again, only now realising that he was still in the Median World. He had no idea how long he had been unconscious and it might have been too late already. Still, he wouldn't be any use to anyone if he stayed dead this time and had to at least try to save himself.

Turning sharply, Richard rushed from the building and ran along the street towards Lancers chapel. As he did he could feel the strength leaving him as the last of his proverbial sands trickled away into the abyss. He could feel the Other Side clutching at him, trying to pull him away, through to the land of the eternally dead.

Still, he continued on, fighting against a rising wind and the cold air of the world darkening around him until, at last, he fell upon the great door to Lancers sanctuary. With the last of his strength he managed to heave open the massive door and, covered with a thick layer of frost which chilled him to the bone, he collapsed before the dull and distant silhouette of Lancer. As he laid there, Lancers shape drifted ever further away, fading into the depths of an unknown reality while the land of death tugged at Richards very soul.

With one last effort, he managed to look up through the snow laden gales that tore at his flesh, blistering it to a burning rawness. A dull glow approached slowly through the blizzard and stood over Richard motionlessly until three words drifted gently through the turmoil, settling softly on his ears..

"Not your time," they stated calmly before Richards grip on the world was lost and he slipped into darkness.

There was an absence of everything. Light, sound, even the unbearable sense of solitude was gone. It was a place of absolute absence, the incarnation of nothing; the Void of Souls.

Supposedly this was the true afterlife, a place where time and space did not exist. A place where even those within did not truly exist to experience it. There *was* something, though, Richard could feel it. Some thread of his being that still clung to the world of the living and refused to let go.

Suddenly streaks of scattered light washed across his vision. They moved so slowly that he could see the particles merge and divide, some swooping majestically as their very structure changed and twisted whilst others swarmed, shattering the fragile waves of their counterparts. Then, just as the particles tried to drift into a veil of impenetrable light, they were pulled away, drawn into an everlasting abyss and, once again, there was nothing.

Richard's eyes flickered open and burned as the buzzing fluorescent light overhead bore down on him. He writhed uncomfortably, clenching his eyelids from the glare. Soon a brightly outlined shadow leant over him, blocking the light to an extent.

"Thought I lost you for a minute there," came Lancers Germanic accent softly, "but that's the last time you're going there, for sure."

Richard sat up uneasily and cradled his spinning head delicately. "I know what you're going to say," he croaked, bodily functions still re-establishing themselves after several hours of being out of use, "I knew the risks after being there so long last time."

"A Median can exist there much longer than anyone else, yes. But the time of every visit is added to the last. Parts of your spirit fall to the Other Side every time-"

"I know!" snapped Richard, sliding himself off the table. "Eventually we all run out of time..." he rubbed his face and steadied himself. "Thank you, though. If you hadn't-"

Lancer turned and put his hand up. "Forget it, you're the one who made it back...What the hell happened out there, anyway?"

Richard paused for a moment and shook his head, barely even believing what he had seen with his own eyes. "Reavers," he managed to state weakly. "They took her and left me for dead. I don't know how long I was out but obviously not as long as they'd hoped."

"No, they don't just leave people. They either take them or kill them outright," he said firmly, rubbing his face in thought. "But that's not the important thing now," he waved his hand dismissively, "we don't know where they have taken her or how to stop Millaian...Or even where to find him for that matter."

Richard reached into his seemingly bottomless pocket and slowly withdrew a half tattered book, streaks of dried blood across its cover. "This is some sort of an adaptation of a notebook he carries around. Don't ask me why but it seems to be really important to him. I don't know why it was made but I'm pretty sure its content is virtually identical," he waved the book around gently. "I think it's somehow got the answer to all this."

"I believed this text to be a myth," Lancer reached for the book and held it carefully, caressing its pages, "and for there to be a copy?" he breathed slowly, gazing at the pages. "I know not how this could have slipped us by," he shook his head and then came to a much more startling enlightenment. "It could not be true that he is the one...The Observer?"

"You mean the madman who went to see the Other Side..." Richard asked coyly, aware of the level of Seer legend they were dealing with, "and come back from it? The one true greatest Seer of all time?" his words were spoken mockingly but not without some degree of reverence.

Lancer nodded shallowly. "Indeed, this is who I speak of. We are told that the unnamed one accomplished many things thought to be impossible for both Seer and Median." Lancer brushed his hand across the cover. "It is said that to achieve these feats he utilised a supposedly magical text named 'Navire.'"

"Vessel," whispered Richard, becoming unsettled by the revelations. "It's possible he isn't. Millaian might be using the Observers work for his own ends..." He stepped out into the open chapel and looked up to the Guardians as if for an answer.

Lancer followed him and pressed his temple, again shaking his head in disbelief. "Matter still stands, if he wasn't then how did he manage to cross over in the first place?" he sighed a breath of begrudging acceptance. "It is him. But no matter what we think of this myth. No matter what other worldly forces or incantations he may wield, Millaian is still just the embodiment of a human based evil, nothing more. The ideal of The Observer remains an inspiration to us all. That we can respect the Other Side and learn to coexist with its spiritual nature," he grinned, reassured of his convictions, even if he was the only one.

"The Other Side..." stated Richard bluntly, still staring at the swirling spectacle of Guardians above. "That's it! That's the answer!" He turned and looked directly at Lancer, his eyes wide open. "You see, we don't even need to confront him. If Millaian is who we think he is and he came back from the Other Side using a ritual in that book," he pointed accusingly at the book in Lancers hand, "then there has to be one that he used to get there in the first place!" He looked away for a few seconds and thought through the idea. "If someone goes and tells on him then," he waved his hands about," whoever is over there might just be able to pull him back. I doubt they're very keen on people escaping."

"No!" Lancer shouted harshly, grabbing Richard by the arm. "There's no way you're going to try this! You have no idea whether there's any help there or if 'there' even exists, for that matter! You've spent too much time in the desert as it is. This could be a one way trip for anyone, let alone you!"

Richard smiled and eased Lancers arm away. "Just as well I've got you here to bring me back then, isn't it?" he smiled again as Lancer lowered his arm and hung his head slightly.

"There never was any stopping you, was there?" he conceded reluctantly, only to be met with another brief smile from Richard. "There is a way…A rite which all Seers know of but for good reason do not know how to conduct," he sighed solemnly for a moment. "We know of it so that if this very text was ever found to be real then it could be destroyed. Such a dangerous power is not meant for anyone of mortal blood lest they fall to the same fate as The Observer," he sighed again heavily, unsure if this was the right course of action. He was, however, acutely aware that it could be their only change to stop Millaian before he unleashed whatever hell he had planned for the world. "It's called The Rite of à L'autre…It translates roughly as 'To the Other,'" he handed the book back to Richard carefully who immediately began riffling through the pages, searching for the incantation. "I have done a terrible thing this day…I have broken the oath of all Seers, what ones that are left anyway. For over a century I have followed my path diligently only for it to come to this."

Richard stopped searching and looked up at Lancer. "I don't believe that…This could have been your path all along…And, if you'll excuse the cliché, you could have just saved all our eternal souls," he went back to searching the book until arriving on one of the last pages. "I think this is it…" he flicked quickly through the book again and returned to the same page. "The Rite of à L'autre et Reconstituer…Looks like it was one of the last he ever used."

Lancer carefully took the book back and gazed at the ritual instructions. "I am not familiar with Reconstituer although I believe it stands to reason that it is a natural part of the ritual that allows the traveller to return to the living world. A part, I feel, that Millaian was unable to use, hence his incarceration in the other world," he rubbed his head briefly in thought. "But how was he able to return at all without this knowledge-?"

"I don't really care," snapped Richard, snatching the book from Lancers hands and quickly reading through the incantation. "We have a chance to stop him without any more bloodshed and that'll do just fine for me," he held up the book and pointed to it firmly. "Do it. Send me to the Other Side."

Lancer opened his mouth loosely, about to reiterate how dangerous the idea was but came to the conclusion that it would be pointless and reluctantly took back the text. "For all it's worth, if you don't come back then I hope you find peace out there somewhere," he spoke the words as softly as he could but only received a simple nod of acknowledgement from Richard.

There was an extended pause before Lancer could bring himself to begin the rite but at last lowered his head and read through the ritual.

"Fire is the key…A doorway, like any element to the many planes of existence." He squinted with effort for a second and waved his hand around a single point in the air. He moved his fingers together into a point and twisted them quickly to spark a small flame that burnt motionless just above his finger tips. "Like the transition between this world and the border, the element must be engaged with. It must be allowed to encompass you and the very essence of what you are. Only then will you have sufficient understanding to proceed…Now, focus on the flame, let it take you away…"

As Richard stared ever deeper into the flame, he could begin to see the true nature of it, the essence that lies beyond normal perception. Slowly his eyes closed with the whispered words flowing from Lancers breath, becoming evermore distant until they were all but gone. His eyes suddenly flicked open again to see a darkened outline of Lancer before him. He still held the flame aloft but now it burnt with an empty shade of blue, its heart darker than the deepest pit. He was back in the border world he knew so well.

"It was so simple…" stated Lancer flatly, "in front of us the entire time…The flame born by the earth, sustained by the air and doused by water. It holds all elementals within its grasp; Birth, life and death," he gazed into the dark flame and smiled. "It's a portal within a portal. The Other Side has always been here, within the flame. The gateway is only our own capacity to see it as such," his voice was full of a fearful glee, as though he were a child toying with something forbidden. "Concentrate again, my friend, and you will see the truth..." Lancer spread his fingers, allowing the flame to move across his palm and waved it before Richard. "Fire is the gateway, the endless portal to the unseen world..." he pressed his palm forward and allowed the dark core to embrace Richard. The world began to fade, eternal night drawing close and just before the starless eternity took him, he heard Lancers final whispered words. "L'eau pour renvoyer la vie...Water to return the life..."

"Can you feel that...? It's the sense of death."
All around there was nothing but darkness and a terrible, chilling cold. Slowly a soft texture took hold, still as cold as before but with a comforting edge that didn't afford the chance to feel alone. It swelled and spread all around, along with it coming a harsh, abrasive wind.

Richard gradually opened his eyes to find himself laid in deep snow with drifts that continued on as far as the eye could see. The blizzard which raged around him, however, ensured that this would not be far at all. Despite this, when he looked skywards, the air was crystal clear allowing him to see a dazzling galactic arc, single stars glittering prominently along its edge.

Richard staggered to his feet, struggling to gain a footing in the soft snow as the gale tried to push him back to the ground. He turned around a few times, trying to see some kind of life or purpose in the windswept tundra but all he found were the faint outlines of twisted, icy forms in the distance, no doubt shaped by centuries of wind and snow. Regardless of the endless stretches of ice and a cold which could freeze a man solid, Richard did not feel the deathly stab of solitude and desperation that he did in the Median World. That voice was with him, even now, the itch of it still in the back of his mind.

"Your time grows short in this place..." it whispered again, "you don't belong here."

Richard swung around and squinted into the snow. "Where are you!?" he shouted at the top of his lungs. "Somehow I don't think this is the Other Side," he added quietly to himself.

"This is true," the whisper seemed to move close and then away as the words were spoken.

"Show yourself," Richard said more calmly, looking up to the celestial horizon again, "I know you're here."

"Our form is beyond your comprehension," it stated one more time, "but we will accommodate if it pleases you."

There were several seconds of complete silence with even the wind seeming to fall quiet while still gusting as strong as it ever had. Soon another outline became apparent in the blizzard, striding closer from the land of ice. It appeared to elevate higher and higher until its shape was far above Richard, positioned atop an icy overhang.

Richard looked around again and now found himself to be surrounded on one side by a sheer glacier wall with nothing behind him but the storm that raged on.

"What is this?" he shouted to the figure with no reply. "Where is this place?"

"You could not be allowed to continue," a deep, gravelly voice eventually came from the overhang, "you would condemn both our worlds."

"This is the Far Side, isn't it? The border world to the Afterlife?" he asked, not quite believing that the place was real.

"You are intelligent yet far from wise. Your incursion on us has damaged the membrane between our worlds. None must travel between worlds unless it is their time!"

"That's why I'm here-" Richard tried unsuccessfully.

"We know why you are here. The one you call Millaian has already breached the membrane. You only weaken it further!" The figure seemed to point accusingly at Richard and then withdraw its arm carefully. "But your intentions are true. You wish to return him to us. I only wish to do the same for you... but I fear you both are now one in the same," he raised an arm as though he was about to swing it.

"Wait!" Richard screamed, raising his hands, submitting. "I only want you to bring him back, stop him from harming my world."

The arm was again lowered, this time more reluctantly. "It is not our place to deal with the matters of your plane, and he is now exactly that." The figure fell silent for a few seconds before crouching and leaning closer, still obscured by the snowy air. "Though we have watched and seen…His ties are of your world, the ones he controls. Separate them and he shall return," he stood again, bolt upright and looked down the cliff. "And so now must you." Quickly he raised and swept his arm harshly in front of Richard calling up a whirlwind which threw him into the night. He managed to look up to the brilliant sky one last time to see the stars streak back into obscurity before otherworldly colours blurred before his eyes. Quickly, he was overcome with a disorientating spinning, a sensation of falling which eventually came to its end with an abrupt jerk.

Slowly Richard opened his eyes and found himself gazing up towards the mass of Guardians swirling around the rafters of Lancers chapel. He gave a gentle sigh of relief and looked about the space. Lancer had placed him on an old mattress in the corner of the main hall. Around him, he realised, were lit candles and burning incense, making the air thick with flavoured smoke. It hung like a fine veil, gently distorting the dull orange light that crept through the stained glass windows.

He sat up, shaking his head at the arrangement. Of course he knew what it was and grimaced at the idea of Lancer having so little faith in him. It was a ritual Seers carried out for those who had passed on, to ease their spirit on its journey to peace.

Richard got to his feet quickly, slightly unsteady after his experience, and strode towards one of the side rooms following the sound of distant voices. As he got closer he found them to be the raised voices of Lancer and Michael, apparently arguing.

"…It is too dangerous! We cannot-!"

"I don't care, it's the only option now!" shouted Michael, cutting off Lancer.

"Do you want all we have accomplished to be for nothing!?" Lancer growled back sternly. "Because without a way to send him back that's exactly what it would all be for."

There was a harsh bang as Michael slammed his hand on a table in frustration. "And if we do nothing then all is lost! We have to confront Millaian and at least try!"

Suddenly the door swung open to reveal Richard standing against the misty air which quickly began spilling into the room. "He's right…We have to confront him now." He smiled at Michael then turned to Lancer seriously, "and I know how to do it," he smiled lightly to himself and stepped further into the room. "We have to exorcise him."

Lancer stared at Richard for quite some time, becoming ever more unsure as the seconds passed. "You're awfully chatty for a dead man."

"Dead?" Richard chuckled. "What makes you think that? I must have only been away an hour, maximum. I mean it's only just dawn now," he waved a hand back at the glow coming through the windows.

Michael and Lancer looked at each other, cautious of how they should proceed. "Rich…I don't know how to tell you this but it's dusk…You've been gone for over 17 hours…" Michael ventured tentatively.

"You see…" Lancer carried on, "after half an hour you still hadn't awoken so I tried the return ritual…It…didn't work," he breathed heavily and shook his head slightly. "I tried it over and over for hours until Michael returned-"

"Which, by the way, is another story entirely," Michael interjected loudly.

"With his information we had a chance but not without you…We tried everything we could Richard, I promise you…But with time running out until All Hallows we finally had to commit ourselves to the idea that you were... gone."

Richard said nothing, trying to comprehend how so much time had passed in this world. The only explanation, he thought, was that considering the time frame of the Median Worlds never seemed to line up with the living world, there must have been a similar effect in the Other Side. The same must have been true for its border world, only much more pronounced. He considered venturing into why this was, what the significance of it had to be but decided he would have to leave the academics for another time. "That doesn't matter now," he tried to convince himself. "What matters is if we have a real chance at stopping him," he looked between the two, each of them still clearly shocked that he was alive. "Now, Michael, what's this information you have?"

"Erm..." he started unsurely, "he found me, Millaian...But I- I managed to get away and found out where he's going," Michael stuttered, thinking it was better he didn't go in to what had really happened.

"He's at the Ansen Memorial...The dome at the centre of the cemetery in town-"

"I know the one," assured Richard quickly, "we should get going now, before it's too late."

"We should take the body, " Lancer stated flatly. "I don't know how much longer she will survive over there. I need to remerge the spirit as soon as possible."

Richard nodded quickly to Michael, prompting him to head outside before turning back to Lancers stone-like features. "Something on your mind?"

"What do you mean by exorcism?" he asked finally after Michael was out of earshot. "Not only is it impossible but the mere idea has been decreed to be forbidden... This whole thing about permanently severing a person from their eternal soul," he clenched his fists and gritted his teeth. "It was never supposed to be done."

"Listen," said Richard firmly, "I never got to the Other Side. I think it was the Far Side border world. Wherever it was, I encountered what I think was their version of a Median. He told me that the only way to defeat Millaian was to separate him from his power...The spirits he controls. The only way to do that is an exorcism. If he won't do it willingly then we have to separate them from him by force," he took a deep, sullen breath. "I don't see there to be any other way."

"There's always another way. Exorcism is wrong-" Lancer tried.

"No!" spat Richard harshly. "The body he controls is not his! He has violated seven people, one of them I consider to be family, and he intends to do it to another before doing god only knows what to everyone else!" He turned away angrily for a few seconds before turning back and pointing a finger accusingly at Lancer. "Your kind! If you had never pushed the boundaries then we would never have be in this goddamn situation!" he breathed heavily, trying to control his temper and eventually lowered his finger. "All you're 'rules'. They don't apply anymore. This is different! Do something right, Lancer. Help me save these people and give them peace."

Lancer stared, furious at Richards outburst before quietly conceding with a gentle sigh. "The process is considered impossible but I suppose you have a way to overturn this assumption, yes?"

"If it's considered so bad, scares Seers so much and has such a strong rule against it then it has to be more than just a theory. Someone must have succeeded in doing it at some point...and I guarantee there's something about it in Millaians book," he looked meaningfully at Lancer, placing a hand on his shoulder. "We chase the extreme, make sure everyone's where their meant to be but, really, nothing's ever just black and white. Sometimes some evil must be done to maintain the greater good."

"That's what I told you, many years ago...It is strange what the student ultimately becomes... and how grateful I am for it," he nodded gently once more and took a deep breath. "Alright, let's do it."

VII - Necrosis

The last enemy that shall be destroyed is death

-Corinthians 15:26

I can't deny that I was scared, more so than I had been in a very long time. If Millaian managed to take Hollie before Midnight then, when the worlds aligned, his true form would return with all the power of the Other Side. I had seen this form. Decades of attempts to return to this world had changed him into a skeletal apparition of twisted humanity. Any sense of the man which had once been was gone. What was left was a creature driven only by a hunger for power, unshackled from what the rest of us would call morality. Yes, I was scared, we all were, but even if I was doing this just to give Chris the peace he deserved then it would have been worth it a thousand times over.

As the veil of the chilled night fell, so did the boundaries between worlds. The planes of the living and dead moving so close that they were capable of imprinting upon each other, going so far as to open fragile portals between them. Usually it was a joyous time for both spirits and the living alike, where reconciliation across the void was possible. A time when long lost relatives could return to their families for a single night.

Tonight was silent, however, for a dark mist hung over both worlds, each knowing that something was coming, one who would defile the sacred time and exploit it as his own.

A car jerked to a halt outside the cemetery gates, mounting the kerb as it did. Quickly, the doors were thrown open and Richard stepped from the driver's side, rushing to assist Michael. Carefully they slid Hollies body from the back seat with Lancer guiding her exit from inside. She had been robed and some colour had returned to her skin although, to anyone looking on, it was clear that she was still dead.

"What time is it?" snapped Richard. "We can't wait any longer."

"Half nine," replied Michael promptly.

"Michael, take her," Lancer passed Hollie into his arms gently and gave Richard a slanted glance. "I'm going to need my hands free if we're going to do this."

Richard glanced back and then at Michael before taking a deep breath and starting towards the large domed building at the centre of the yard. There was a small opening to the crypt, covered with a slightly ajar wooden door. Richard looked back at the others and slowly pressed it open into the damp gloom of the age old tomb.

All around were shadowed alcoves with skeletons lying therein, each with an engraved plaque above. They lined the walls row upon row atop each other and in the centre stood a raised platform where Millaian crouched, eyes closed, chanting quietly to himself.

The repeated, incoherent words were enough to strike a chill through Richards nerves. Even so, he slowly stepped towards the platform, looking closer at his seemingly unaware foe.

"Can't be that easy," he whispered to himself, gazing at Millaian's figure hunched in the hazed darkness. He turned back and waved Lancer towards him, speaking in low tones as to try and avoid drawing attention to themselves. "I guess now's as good a time as any."

"I'm sure it is," Lancer quipped back, walking gingerly up the shallow steps of the circular platform. Coming within a few feet of Millaian, he drew a deep breath and took his final step forward, rigidly reaching out an open and shaking hand.

Lowering his head and closing his eyes he placed his hand within half an inch of the decomposing skull and started to mumble repeated words in Latin. His words slowly began to overpower Millaians continued chant and a dull, ultraviolet glow began to creep from beneath his hand. Starting to smile with his success, Lancer stated the words over and over with ever growing confidence. As he did, the glow continued to spill over Millaian, creating a pool of almost unseen light on the ground around them.

Suddenly the light vanished, along with Lancers sense of nearing victory, as Millaians eyes flicked open and his teeth began to grit against his exposed jaw.

Lancer removed his hand, clenching it tightly as Millaian rose before him. "Oh no," he whispered gently just as he was thrown back down the steps.

Millaian rose his arms, calling forth a shimmering wave which rippled through the air, knocking everyone before him to the ground and illuminating the crypt with a brilliant light.

Slowly the light began to fade and Richard looked about, blinking, eyes stinging as his sight returned to him. At first he thought it to be his eyes adjusting but as he was assured they had returned to normal, it became apparent that the entire crypt was lit with an otherworldly glow. It was not just as if a light were now shining but every wall, every surface now shined with a pale, sickly radiance. He looked around again for Michael and Lancer but they were gone. The only one who remained was Millaians true, twisted form atop the platform, glowing brighter than the rest of the crypt.

There was silence for several seconds as Millaian stood motionless, the atmosphere around him appearing to be drift like an early morning mist. "Such ignorance," he stated in a hollow, terror inducing tone, "you're failure shows your weakness..." He leaned forward, every part of his tall, lean body moving distinctly to the next, giving his movement a serpentine quality. "It is futile to use my own incantations against me...for I am immune." He straightened back up again and grinned a terrible, toothy grin, the sight juxtaposed awkwardly against his washed out, withered face. "You have not the intelligence to devise something original. This you have already proven."

"I demand you give her back to this world and return to your own!" shouted Richard, getting to his feet. "I know what you are and you cannot remain here anymore!"

Millaian grimaced slightly, almost grinning at Richards's statement. "That's exactly what he said…Just as he let me slip away into that hell. You know nothing about me!" He stepped off of the platform, his tattered cloak flowing weightless behind him, and slowly began to move towards Richard. "I do know much about you, however, and for that reason I have already triumphed," he grinned again, turning around and heading back to the platform.

Richard watched the hollow being for a while and then decided to take a bold step. "Christophe Guillaume…" he stated flatly, making Millaian stop abruptly and swing around. "He was the one, wasn't he? The one who couldn't let you do those things anymore. He knew this would happen so after you were gone he took your notebook and published it so that there was at least a chance to stop you."

"That book is nothing…Just words. Mine has innate power, merged to my very being. It awoke me and at last I could be rid of that wretched text." He stared sternly but something in his face gave away a humanity that still resided deep within him. Merely hearing Christophe's name had invoked a pain inside of him. Richard imagined that having to use the published work to conduct his deeds, the very thing intended to betray him, hurt more than any hell he spoke of. "You remind me of him," Millaian said softly at last, "that is why I brought you here…I wished you to be the first I destroy when I reclaim my dominion."

"Reclaim your dominion?" repeated Richard disapprovingly. "You never had one in the first place! By all accounts you died. Committed suicide because life got too much for you."

"Exactly what I intended the weak minded to think," he straightened up to his full height and began to laugh hauntingly. "I could not go on living a normal life, constantly seeing these things! After my supposed death I travelled to France and spent years working with the best Median I could find trying to discover the truth of life and existence its self…"

"Christophe," Richard said gently.

"Yes. But I eventually came to realise there is nothing! Nothing at all...Only power. Power the strong should take and the weak should obey! My old friend... He did not see it as such. He lied to me each and every day, gained my trust and, when we were so close to the end, betrayed me!" Millaian threw his arm down in disgust and growled darkly. "Never again. This time my victory will be complete." There was a shimmer in the air beside him and a shape began to form. It wavered and rippled until it was all but discernible.

"Hollie!" Richard tried to rush forward but was stopped as more figures started to appear all around him. Somehow they were Reavers. He tried to take in the situation for a moment, then made a stark realisation. "This is a Merge, isn't it? A point between the worlds that become one in the same? But only for tonight? "

Millaian nodded and opened a bony hand towards Hollie. "Blood is thicker than water, as they say. Her blood is very thick indeed. It shall be my conduit to this world..." He turned his head towards her with a crack and gazed down on her with deep set eyes. "My lineage is strong in you."

"No," said Hollie softly, "I can't be." Her lip began to tremble and her breath grew rapid with morbid terror.

"Millaian!" shouted Richard again, past the Reavers. "I'm giving you one last chance! Stop this and return to the Other Side!"

He laughed again with the Reavers looking back, as if surprised he could do such a thing. "You have no way to command me...I do as I please."

Richard chuckled lightly as there was a change in the air. "Then you should have killed me sooner," he said quietly. "Lancer only began the process. Now the worlds have merged, I can finish it." He looked up at Hollie, "only I'm not leaving without her."

Millaian looked down upon him, bewildered at what he saw as a mere insect, as Richard bowed his head and closed his eyes.

"*Libertas tua est, amici mei.*" The words echoed around the building and fell gently upon all who heard it like a fresh spring rain until it faltered and finally drifted away to nothing.

"That's it?" said Millaian harshly. "Latin?"

Richard lifted his head again, opening his eyes. "I command you..." he raised his hand to the sprawling crowd of Reavers before him. "Leave this place." The words moved forward with no force or malice, only the pure assurance of a clear mind capable of directing the spirits that walked his world.

As each comprehended the meaning of the words, they turned and vanished into the ether. "You choose to bring this to my plane and so I will use the power I have on this night alone to command all who would infringe on the living. On this night I decree..." he started walking towards Millaian as the last remnants of the Reavers vanished into mist, "freedom is yours."

There was silence for a few seconds and Millaian was about to belittle Richards' attempts at grandeur. He was stopped when Hollie too gasped and vanished into to a mist which drifted towards the door where her body had been dropped.

As she went, a single word echoed back through the air, "life."

Milliaian went to open his dried lips to speak again but instead slowly looked around to six pale and translucent figures standing behind him. As he looked from one to the next, each began to dissolve away in turn, leaving only a fading imprint in the air.

"Your power has gone, you have no choice anymore," Richard continued softly. "Leave this place."

While Richard spoke, Millaian fell to his knees, gritting his teeth as he tried to hold on to the world but with every passing second another part of his spirit slipped away.

"I cannot be destroyed," he managed to say, his gravelly voice broken by laboured gasps. "I will have my triumph!" he growled finally before clutching his chest and exploding outwards into a dark powder that drifted to the ground, fizzling as it did.

Richard took a deep sigh and rubbed his face, hardly able to believe that it may just be over.

"Thank you," came a gentle feminine voice from the platform, making Richard look up again. It was one of the spirits who Millaian had enslaved, still standing in place where the rest had left. "For everything you have done, we wish to give you this," she smiled brightly before lowering her head and vanishing like the others leaving the distorted but solid shape of Chris behind her.

"It can't be..." Richard walked, unfaltering towards him, "are you-"

"Real?" finished Chris, his shape becoming truer as the spirits imprint faded. "As real as I can be," he looked around at the building, its walls beginning to fade back to their normal colour. "They pulled you over to the border but I still don't have long. The worlds are already beginning to move apart and we are on different sides of a *vast* divide." He nodded towards the doorway, calling Richards attention to Michael and Lancers faint, ghostly figures tending to Hollie as she started to sit up. They turned and looked at Chris' mangled body lying just at the feet of Richards astral figure, unable to believe it was done.

"So much to say…" tried Richard. "Stay with us."

"I can't," he looked down at his feet and the mutilated body of his real self, "but you can join me. Your time in the mortal realm has been honourable but now it is time to leave," he reached forward a hand. "Come and you will see a world beyond your imagination."

Richard looked down, thinking for a second and slowly began to raised his arm, stretching it out to take Chris's hand.

Behind him, Hollie watched Richards spectre begin to fade and quickly pushed Michael and Lancer away, getting up to rush towards him. Distraught, she tried to reach for him but soon stopped and took a deep breath, realising why everything had happened to her. Just as Michael had, she took the final step of understanding and embraced what she truly was. As she did she stepped across the divide, becoming as much a phantom as those before her.

"Richard," she spoke as though she had known him for years and reached for his shoulder, causing him withdraw his hand from Chris. "You can't do this. I know now that the world still needs you…They need you," she waved her hand back towards the other two and looked around unsurely, "and I think I'll need you…Please, don't leave us."

Something told Richard that he should listen to her. Now, after all these years of feeling alone, he realised he always had people all along, people who cared for him and could understand everything he went through. He looked mournfully to the fading figure of Chris and shook his head gently. "I'm sorry, I have to stay."

Chris said nothing but merely gave a shallow nod and a gentle smile.

"I hope you find her…" Richard added finally.

Chris' image had almost dwindled away to nothing but just before he vanished completely, whispered words drifted across the divide. They simply stated, "look after him."

With the living world returning to normal around them, Richard looked to Hollie and smiled. She barely knew these people but somehow felt everything had changed. Instead of saying anything she merely smiled back as Michael and Lancer finally joined them.

The sun slowly rose over a world oblivious to how close it had come to anarchy, Richard, Michael and Hollie walked along a damp street as the lights overhead flicked off from another night of illuminating the shadows.

Hollie looked down at the robe she was still wearing. "I should really get some clothes if I'm going to be alive again, you know," she stopped and thought for a second. "Come to think of it what's going to happen to me? Everyone thinks I'm dead."

"Don't worry," said Richard reassuringly, "I have some contacts. They can make it look like a clerical error in hospital paperwork, everyone else will just dismiss it. I've found people have short memories. Now the Reavers are gone, everything will be back to normal for you in no time."

"Oh, I don't think things will ever be normal again after this," she chuckled brightly and moved closer to him. "Honestly, I don't think I'd have it any other way."

"Question is…" started Richard suspiciously, "how did Michael get away from Millaian?"

Michael stopped, sighing and turned to Richard. "My father," he said, startling Richard somewhat. "I know it was Chris... When Millaian had me pinned, I think he took control somehow, stopped him from killing me. Instead he just knocked me out," he clutched his head and shook it briefly. Gave me one hell of a headache, but I'm alive, at least."

"Family's a powerful thing," Hollie offered reassuringly.

"As for the cemetery, don't ask me how I know he'd be there. When I woke up, I just knew where he was going to be... like I just knew that I was a Median…"

Richard nodded uneasily. "Family's a powerful thing..."

I wasn't about to question what he had said. I had always known just to respect the old ways and this latest incident had driven that home all too well. I'm glad he knew about Chris now. He was a good man who succumb to the pressure of too many worlds on his shoulders, the fate of all too many good Medians. I think Lancer learnt a thing or two about his kin as well, although it surprises me to think that a century old Seer could still be so deeply shaken by new revelations. It just goes to prove that no matter what we think we know, there will always be more to this universe than meets the eye. It was something Michael would come to learn very soon for the true meaning of what it meant to be a Median ran far deeper than even I could possibly understand. One thing was sure, though, Hollie was right when she said that things wouldn't go back to normal. Something tells me that, after all this, nothing will be the same again... for any of us.

Printed in Great Britain
by Amazon

11054995R00058